HEAR ME BABY, HOLD TOGETHER

HEAR ME BABY SERIES
BOOK 1

JEFF SILVEY

FEAR &
MERCY
PUBLISHING

Published in the United States by Fear and Mercy Publishing, Austin, Texas. Visit the author's website at jeffsilvey.com

Library of Congress Control Number: 2025912218

ISBN: 978-1-968557-00-3 (paperback)

Some roads lead away from home—others lead straight into the fire.

June Addison should have graduated by now. At nineteen, she's stuck repeating high school in Vacaville, California—a sun-baked town where secrets fester behind picket fences. Her best friend dreams of freedom. June just wants to survive the week.

At home, June keeps quiet and leaves her bedroom door unlocked. Her mother's boyfriend, Randy, won't allow otherwise. He watches. Waits. And now he's crossed a line she can't ignore. Her mother looks the other way. Her best friend wouldn't understand. And June is running out of places to hide.

As the summer heat intensifies, so does the pressure. June must decide how far she's willing to go to protect herself—and what she's willing to leave behind.

Meanwhile, in Santa Fe, a new security guard takes a quiet job at a government lab buried beneath the desert. But the deeper he goes, the more he sees, and the harder it gets to look away. Before long, he's caught in something far bigger than he signed up for, with no clear way out.

Told through converging storylines, *Hear Me Baby, Hold Together* is a tense, emotionally charged thriller about people trapped by circumstances beyond their control, the price of survival, and the courage it takes to break free—even when escape might cost them everything.

To the survivors,
hold on, there's always a way

HEAR ME BABY, HOLD TOGETHER

DRIVE

DECEMBER 13, 1989
INTERSTATE 15
CALIFORNIA–NEVADA BORDER

June Addison grips the steering wheel until her knuckles throb. This could all be a big mistake. The thought circles her mind like a vulture as she creeps along the nearly empty highway, her foot barely brushing the accelerator. Why did she ever agree to this trip? She'd driven through the night once before in a car just like this one, and it wasn't any easier to handle.

She's not good with cars, or boys, for that matter. But then *he* came into her life. This beast is his baby. A finely refurbished something-or-other; the exact name escapes her. All she knows about the car is that it is his undying obsession. It's almost enough to make her jealous.

The truth is, he loves this car more than anything, and she loves seeing him happy. Those rare moments when his wry smirk becomes something real; the veil lifts back and she can see him, the real him. Though he only appeared in her life two weeks ago, it feels like she's known him all along. The one thing that makes everything all right has just fallen into her lap.

They don't make them like this anymore—the car or the boy. Or is it man? Boys are over; high school ended for her a long time ago. The real world is full of men with their grown-up toys. Like this damn car. It's the only thing she doesn't like about John, and it was almost a deal-breaker: a black muscle car with two vertical white stripes running down the hood and an engine that sounds like a lion's roar.

Douchemobile.

That's what she would have called it before, cooing the words to her best friend as they giggled together on their way to school. Back when she still had a friend. Back before her life fell apart.

So much has changed since that summer night when it all began. She can pinpoint the exact moment when she realized her mother had been lying to her for so long. June pulled the thread, and her whole world unraveled. Since then, it's only been about survival; and tonight, to get through this, she'll have to stay awake and in her own lane on this never-ending dark highway. Crashing into the ditch that runs along this stretch of I-15 is probably not the best way to start a new relationship. If this even is a relationship; she still doesn't know what to call this thing that came out of nowhere and turned her life upside down and inside out.

This dark-haired man with his relentless smile appeared in the restaurant where she worked, and it was like seeing the sun for the first time. They didn't even speak, only noticed each other from across the dining room. When she saw his face, his smile, his eyes—the world reduced itself to a pinhole. Life suddenly became so clear. There was simply what mattered and what didn't.

They were inseparable for the next two weeks. She knew better, but she couldn't help herself. It wasn't fair, John disarming her with that constant grin of his. He was on a short stint in Southern California doing whatever it was he did for a living, something to do with insurance companies and lawyers, tall buildings and big terrible accidents. Then it came, as they both knew it would—his last day. He was getting ready to say goodbye, to move on to the next city and the next catastrophic liability. She would never see him again. But just when she was about to say goodbye, he turned to her, looking like the Cheshire Cat.

"Hey, I could blow off this next job. Want to go to Vegas?"

"You're kidding, right?" She laughed and smiled back.

His eyes narrowed, and he asked it again, adding the question that (at her age) was the go-to excuse for everything. "Why not? Who knows, there could be a nuclear war and the world could end tomorrow."

And it wasn't really his face—his kind eyes, upturned mouth, and cleft chin—but rather his attitude, his pure assurance that life would be good and everything would be fine, come what may.

Her heart skipped a beat as her mind raced. Did she still have money in her account? Could she get some time off on such short notice? This was it, the kind of thing she dreamed about—a once-in-a-lifetime flash, the moment she would look back on later in life and say, "That was when everything changed."

It wasn't long before they were rolling toward Nevada's most famous city, John driving with the radio on full blast, both of them shouting—"Woo-hoo, Vegas!"—at the top of their lungs.

When things quieted down and John started nodding off, June made him stop in Barstow to stretch his legs. She offered to drive; it took several tries, but he finally relented. And now here he is, sawing logs with his face leaning against the passenger side window, drool running down his chin, his head bobbing with every slight dip in the road.

Even though the speed limit is 70, June doesn't want to push her luck; this car has too much torque for her to handle. She mentally whispers an apology to Sammy Hagar as she cruises along at a safe 55 miles per hour.

The only other car on the road has been tailgating her for the last five miles. A beat-up white Honda Accord with an over-weight red-haired man behind the wheel. He gives her the finger as he finally passes her in the fast lane. June doesn't care; he can have the road. Right now she's got what she wants, with all the time in the world, or so she tells herself. The truth is, there's only one more week left until the man she adores will walk right out of her life, probably forever. Her life is a mess; she can't plan more than three hours ahead on any given day. The concept of forever is like Chinese algebra to her. All she knows is right now she gets a dream week with him in Vegas, take it or leave it.

She'll take it.

She eases off the gas and tries to relax her grip, the floor-boards rumbling beneath her black-and-white Chuck Taylors. The ensuing quiet gives her too much time to think. Fidgeting, she pulls out a cigarette and lights it with the dash-mounted lighter, its coils glowing bright red. At least this old car is good for something.

Thoughts of that other car, the one like this from so long ago, keep coming back. The time she drove all night, headlights cutting through the darkness. She didn't know what to do and had nowhere to go, couldn't see the road through her own tears.

That car smelled like *him*, the Big Bad Him and his bullshit Drakkar he doused himself with whenever he went out; though the stench was bad enough, it wasn't the worst part—she'll never forget the horror she found in the trunk.

June takes a slow drag off her cigarette and blows the smoke out her slightly open window. No matter how bad things got, she remained a survivor. She had to keep telling herself to hold on, there's always a way, and it's worked out so far.

She looks over at John and smiles. Damn this man. He made

her take this trip. When she was trying to make up her mind, he was already on the phone making plans. This is a man who knows what he wants and knows exactly how to get it. She longs for that—to be so sure of herself, so comfortable in her own skin. Being around him is intoxicating. She has to get to know him better. Is he always like this? What's the secret of this strange mystery man who walked into her life on one cold winter's morning and changed everything?

She only learned his last name yesterday: Pearce. John Pearce. Though he is in his mid-twenties, he walks like an old soul and lives in a state of perpetual relaxation, always knowing what to do or say wherever he finds himself. What's that like? June has no idea. She worries over everything, the poster child for social awkwardness.

She bites her lip. Lying to John was a mistake. She's always believed that withholding the truth is the same as lying, and she hasn't been completely honest with him. But he can't find out her whole story, not yet. She can't risk losing him when it feels like her life is just beginning.

She puts the cigarette to her lips and inhales one last time, letting the smoke burn her throat. She winces but welcomes the pain as some kind of twisted penance for her lie. As she flicks the butt out the window, her eyes hover over the side mirror. A police car is keeping pace right behind her.

"Shit."

She glances back in the rearview, thinking maybe she got it wrong, maybe the anxiety of the drive is just playing tricks on her mind. But no, there it is: black-and-white car, square head-lights, light bar across the roof. How could she have missed it?

Her pulse quickens. How long has he been there? Would he stop someone for driving too slowly? Did he see her throw that cigarette out the window? She's not sure if that's a crime on the highway. It's not like they're in the middle of a grassy field.

The lights come on from behind, and her vision clouds over

with red and blue swirls. June's head spins and her stomach tightens. Then something far worse hits her, something she's been running from for the past six months: They found her! After all she's been through, this is how it's going to end. They're going to put her away for life.

The cop speeds up and gets into the fast lane. Pulls up next to her. Time stops. All sound is sucked out of the world, leaving her in a vacuum, her ears ringing in the silence. There he is, the cliche in front of her eyes—mirrored sunglasses, brown mustache, smug look on his face. June can't breathe.

He turns to face her, gives her a nod and a quick salute with the top two fingers of his right hand; his mouth parts, and the word is there in her mind: *Ma'am*. His siren blares and he continues on, speeding off into the distance.

June sighs. Her hands shake as she closes the window and adjusts her hair in the rearview mirror. Thinking music might soothe her frazzled nerves, she reaches down and turns on the radio. It's like an explosion, a sudden clash of drums and guitar from some classic rock station John left on too loud. She curses and punches off the radio as fast as she can.

John stirs and lifts his head, his eyes bleary. He mumbles something incoherent.

"Sorry," June says. "Radio helps when I'm anxious."

"Anxious?" John sits up. "From going on a trip with a guy you barely know?"

"Just excited, babe."

"Me too. Pull over, I'll drive the rest of the way."

SIX MONTHS EARLIER...

1

NERVOUS IN SUBURBIA

JUNE ADDISON TURNS to lie on her stomach, her yellow beach towel crunching on the dry grass beneath her. It is another hot day in Vacaville, California—105 degrees and rising, and with no clouds in the sky, there is nothing to stop the sun from baking everything in sight. Though extreme, this is nothing new. May fed into June with an incessant heatwave that is likely to last all summer. As bad as it is, the weather is the least of June's worries.

At least she's not alone. Her best friend—Bree Montgomery—invited herself over again, even though her parents have a giant house and an even bigger pool. Since this is the Sunday before the last week of school, the girls are doing the only thing there is to do on a torrid afternoon like this: spend their time sunbathing and swimming and talking about boys.

Bree is up on her elbows, her chin in her hands, being a chatterbox, as usual, going on about some apparently hilarious party she went to last night. As complicated as high school can be, the one thing you can always count on is that if a party was going down on Saturday night, Bree Montgomery was there. Her legs kick up and down as she works herself into a frenzy.

"So I'm standing at the fridge, and there's only one wine

cooler left. Todd is totally reaching for it. You know Todd, from third period history? The one with the glasses? I turn to him and I'm like, 'Whoa, dude, you just got here. You're like, totally sober. But look, I've had a few, I'm *feeling* it.'

"He just looks at me like I'm crazy, but I know he's kind of a pushover. So I go, 'Come on, it's just one, and that's all we got left. Look, man, if you take this, you won't feel a thing. But if I drink it, I'm going to get *more buzzed*. Think about it.'

"He actually scratches his head. I know, right? I give him my big girlie smile and say, 'Seriously, Todd, who could use this more?' And he just stands there like an idiot, so I grab that fucking Seagrams and leave him holding his dick."

June's eyes open wide.

"So to speak!"

"Oh, Bree, can't take you anywhere."

"Can't take *me* anywhere? At least I go out. Where were you?" Bree says. "Should've been there, girl. Todd's a dork, but there were some cuties in the house. You know what they say."

Not really, June thinks. She picks at the cuticle on her right thumb. She can't stand all the endless talk about how much everyone drinks. When June was sixteen, a drunk driver totaled her father's car, and ever since then she's equated drinking with being an asshole. Never again. Being in a house full of people getting sloppy would make her feel like spiders were crawling all over her skin.

June can't blame Bree right now, though. She's excited. Who wouldn't be? She's about to graduate from Vaca High and is making plans to move away at the end of the summer. She and her parents are currently waiting for acceptance letters from several colleges; her top two choices are UCLA in Los Angeles and USF in San Francisco. Bree is bursting with anticipation as she counts down the days until fall. June does her best to hide her annoyance.

At nineteen, June is two years older than her best friend, yet she still has her senior year ahead of her. Being older than her classmates makes her self-conscious and awkward in social situations. When nervous, she compulsively touches the burn scars on her left shoulder, which only draws more attention to herself. She doesn't go out much on weekends, except to the movies or to the mall with Bree.

She lets her mind wander while Bree continues her diatribe. June loves her, but damn, it's hard to think around her sometimes. June has always believed the good things in life are inherently simple: a quiet moment, like now, with the sun sparkling and dancing on top of the pool, the light moving in waves as the water ripples with the breeze. Bree, however, is a drama queen; nothing is ever simple with her. They are opposites in many ways, but maybe that's what June likes about Bree. She keeps life interesting.

What's it going to be like when her only friend moves away? Could things really get any worse?

The truth is, life in the Addison household has taken a bizarre, dark turn, and June is having a hard time broaching the subject with her friend, the party girl, whose biggest problem in life is choosing a nail polish to match her outfit. June has to say something, or she'll go crazy. She takes a deep breath, but when fear makes her hesitate, Bree blurts out again.

"They say he's into himself, but…"

Bree's mouth is in constant motion—her full lips moving up and down, then opening wide to let out her high-pitched laugh. Always happy, always enjoying the moment. More often than not, June can't help but laugh along with her.

No, Bree's not so bad. She's a wonderful distraction, which is what June needs right now. June doesn't want to think too much. If you look too hard, you might notice things that don't make sense. Sometimes, especially when things are beyond your control, it's best to put your head down and simply trudge ahead. Her mother used to have a calendar on the kitchen wall that featured a cartoon laborer taking a big step forward. The caption underneath read: *Keep On Keeping On!*

Sometimes that's all you can do. Sometimes that's enough.

Bree groans and rolls onto her back. "…okay, I admit it, that's all true. But he's the hottest guy in fourth period."

Pregnant pause. That's a prompt, June knows. She doesn't answer, just lets the moment hang, listening to the sparrows chirping in the breeze behind her. So alive, so innocent.

"Hey, are you okay?" Bree asks.

"Yeah, why?"

"You've been quiet all afternoon."

"Can I tell you something?" June says, closing her eyes. This is it, finally a chance to tell someone what's really going on in this messed-up family. Her mother puts on a good front whenever anyone else is around, so things must look fine to an outsider, but June is miserable. She needs to make sure it's not all in her head.

A car drives by, not far beyond the brown wooden fence surrounding the backyard. Tires grip pavement at the stop sign, then squeal as the driver guns it down Greeley Street.

"Boys," June says matter-of-factly. Too many boys with so much to prove. A common occurrence in Cowtown. June means the car, but Bree takes it literally. As in *boys*. As in *lack thereof*.

"Oh, Junie, what are we gonna do?"

There it is, Bree's undying loyalty. It's always "we," always "us." June loves her for it. It's nice to have at least one person you can always count on—well, one person besides your family. Your family has to be there for you, that's a given. But June only knew that feeling for a brief time in her young life. Everything changed when her father died. Now she can't count on anyone but her best and only friend.

Bree continues in a desperate voice. "Another week? I don't think I can take another *day* of school. Kill me. Why can't it be the Golden Week right now?"

June lays her head flat against her arms and says into her towel, "Soon, Bree. Real soon."

It is the irony of summer. Although they both have three months off from school, they spend most of their time working. It happens every year: Bree is a cashier at a clothing store on the outskirts of town, and June is a hostess at Vaca Pete's, a family restaurant just off Main Street. Not content with the meager time together their busy schedules allowed, the girls made a sacred pact, and thus, the Golden Week was born. Every year, at least until one of them leaves for college, they both take the same week off and spend it doing whatever they want.

Ah, the glorious Golden Week, a blissful respite with no responsibilities, when they can pretend to be thirteen again. Unfortunately, this year a horrible truth threatens to cast a shadow over their halcyon days.

"I hate to say it," June begins.

"Then don't say it," Bree says, her eyes closed under her sunglasses, her face turned toward the sun.

June whispers, "It looks like Creepy Randy is going to be here all month. And yeah, *that* week, too."

Bree sighs. "He's going to ruin everything."

"Let's keep our voices down," June says. "I don't know if he's still home. He might hear us."

Randy Volker is her mother's boyfriend and June's most hated enemy. They moved in with him last year, and he's been tormenting June ever since. She tries to spend as little time with him as possible, and when he's around, she invokes her golden rule for dealing with useless and mean authority figures: Speak only when spoken to.

Fortunately, he is away for long stretches of time on business trips that take him all over California and the greater Southwest. His absences are met with smiles from June and indifference from her mother. Though not imposing in stature, Randy is ruth-less with those he deems weaker than himself, which regrettably includes June. It's easy for her to see through his overbearing discipline and know him for the bully he truly is, but her mother always seems oblivious, as if her own little world doesn't extend that far, can't include those colors of aggression and cruelty.

His behavior toward June took an odd turn about five months ago. For no apparent reason, he began to act differently —nice is not the right word, and he is incapable of being truly kind. In his own way, he was more attentive and present.

What should have been a welcome change only struck June as an insult. It felt all wrong. He was anathema to her; his mere presence made her skin crawl. Every look Randy gave her was like an unyielding leer. Now she can't stand to be in the same room with him. Her mother, on the other hand, continues to act as if everything is fine. June thinks she must be going crazy.

This can't be normal. She has to talk to Bree about it, get her take on this. June suddenly feels sick to her stomach. She knows if she doesn't say something soon, she might never build up the nerve again. Thankfully, Bree's incessant monologue is coming to an end.

"... so I said goodbye to Lance and his grabby hands and booked it to my car." Bree puts her hand to her head. "Seriously, ugh!"

So dramatic, but the pause gives June an opening. She blurts out the words before she can think twice. "Hey, look, speaking of grabby hands—"

"I know, right?" Bree leans over and playfully pushes June's shoulder. "Last week I had to bail when Mike Daten kept staring at me like I was a CPR dummy. So gross, he tries to make out with any girl with a pulse. He's probably got like mouth herpes or something."

June's heart sinks. She sighs loudly, and Bree doesn't even

notice. Time for a break. She stands and gestures toward the pool. "I'm going in. Coming?"

Bree adjusts her mirrored sunglasses. "No, maybe later."

June stands on the diving board, the sun's intense rays scorching her shoulders. She closes her eyes and soaks in the searing heat, then leans forward and plunges into the pool with a splash. The arctic water shakes her whole being; the familiar sensation awakens something in her.

She comes up and gasps for air. The chlorine smell reminds her of when she was a little girl taking her first swimming lessons at the county pool. Shy in her Disney princess swimsuit —with the instructors trying to coax her to jump in by herself— she was always too afraid to move, let alone jump into the scary, huge pool. She cried the first few times, but her father was always there to calm her down and make her feel safe.

Though she often feels like one, she's not a little girl anymore; she's not even the same person. The neon tankini she wears now hides most of the burn scars that run down the left side of her torso, leaving only her shoulder scars visible. The cut on her right cheek? Well, there's nothing she can do about that. Too self-conscious, she only wears a swimsuit in her own back-yard, much to Bree's dismay. Never that modest, Bree could walk around in a bikini all day; she would wear one to church if she could.

June wipes the water from her eyes and looks over at her best friend, who is spilling out of little green triangles that don't cover nearly enough. It's hard not to resent her. Bree is young and blonde, with a special charisma that exudes confidence and finesse. Her parents, who are supportive to an almost ridiculous degree, let her do whatever she wants. They probably don't even know where she is right now.

What's that like? June can't imagine. Why can't she be normal for once in her life? Bree is the only person June can trust, but the thought of explaining any of this to her is over-whelming. Bree just won't get it. How could she?

June paddles to the shallow end and stands up, twirling her long hair to squeeze the water out. A natural dirty blonde, she dyed it a deep red for the summer. Her mother frowned, quick to express her disappointment, but this was nothing new. It seems every time June does something to improve herself, her mother is there poised and ready with words that sting, the venom lingering long after the dust settles on any argument between them.

With a mother like that, June needs Bree at her side now more than ever. She shifts gears and lets her damp hair fall to her shoulders, giving her friend a faux-sexy look.

Bree laughs and calls out, "How is it, Buttercup?"

"It's nice. Why don't you cool off before you burn up?"

"Why don't you come over here and tell me about your new little boyfriend?"

"You know I don't have a boyfriend." June grabs the ladder to pull herself up and out of the pool. "I'd be in a much better mood if I had a boyfriend."

"For sure." Bree smiles mischievously. "Girl, we have to get you laid. Oh, I know, let's go to the movies Friday night. *Bill & Ted* is playing at the Dollar Theater. I'll get Bobby to take me, we just need to find you a date."

"Sounds like you've got it all worked out."

Bree looks at June out of the corner of her eye and gives her a wry smile. "Make your own luck, that's what I always say."

"You're a real piece of work, my friend," June giggles. A night at the movies is a welcome fantasy, but after the last fight with her mother, June can only hope that she'll be let out of the house at all during the Golden Week, let alone this Friday night. Of course, with Randy home, you never know. Mommy dearest might forget June exists.

"We'll see," June says. "But you'll have to drive. My car is still tits up. Randy said he could fix it, but he's taking forever."

"Is he really going to be home all month?" Bree asks.

"Looks like it. For a few weeks, at least. Creep. I better get my car back soon, and if he craps on our Golden Week, I'm going ballistic."

Without thinking, Bree glances at the large sliding glass door on the back patio. The blinds are drawn, but they flutter when she turns her head to look, as if someone inside had just been peeking through them. Even in the blazing sun, a shiver runs down her spine. "Creep indeed. D-bag, if you ask me. Hey, why do you still have that piece of crap, anyway?"

Bree never liked June's car. A 1978 Volkswagen Bug, light blue, with a big scratch across the front door and too many dents to count.

June's pulse races as a wave of anger washes over her. The car was a gift from her late father; in fact, it was the last thing he gave her before he died. She closes her eyes and lets the feeling pass. She doesn't want to fight with Bree, not when they have something so important to talk about. Drawing a deep breath, she takes the high road.

"How dare you," she says with fake sarcasm. "I love that car. It's my first, and you never forget your first."

"Hmmm," Bree pretends to think, then adds suggestively, "and do you remember *your* first?"

"Ew, gross." June lowers her sunglasses to her nose. "I don't have a first like that, thank you very much."

"I wish you did," Bree says in a sing-song voice. "You'd have much more interesting stories to tell, thank you very little."

Unfortunately, June only has horrible stories to tell, stories about her mother's live-in boyfriend with wandering hands and no concept of boundaries. The thought of it all makes her dizzy. Doubt clings to her like a second skin. What if she's wrong? What if it's nothing after all and she really is crazy? She's afraid of what Bree will say. What if Bree laughs or thinks differently about her? What if she tells everyone at school? But June can't keep up this indecision forever. She'll explode.

Unable to hold back, the words pour out. "Randy's been seriously freaking me out lately. No, for real. He won't let me lock any doors anymore—not my bedroom, not even the bathroom. Last week, I was in the shower, and he just barged into the bathroom. He was going on about some dumb new rule, like I have to do the dishes every night or whatever. We have this little stool thing by the toilet. He dragged it over and stood on it, looking right down at me. I tried to cover up, but he just kept talking, asking if I understood."

"Understood what?"

"Whatever stupid rule he was going on about. I mumbled something, and he finally left. I kept the water running and cried for like ten minutes. That can't be normal." She leans in closer. "I mean, that's not okay, right?"

"Yeah," Bree says, still on her back, looking up at the sky. "Rules are bullshit. My dad never lets me talk on the phone after nine at night. I swear, he's literally Hitler."

June wants to cry. It's not Bree's fault; her perfect little life gives her no context for understanding any of this. And once again, June finds herself alone, like she's overboard and lost at sea, too tired to keep treading water, just waiting for the current to pull her under.

Frustrated, she stands and grabs her towel, wrapping it around her waist. "I'm going inside for a Coke. Want anything?"

Bree grunts a negative response and closes her eyes.

She'll be asleep in a few minutes, June thinks. I better come back and check on her soon. Don't want her to burn all to hell.

June opens the sliding glass door and walks into the family room, annoyed that she has to brush past the closed curtains. A strange yellowish tint fills the room from the shades drawn on all the windows. She scrunches her face as her defenses go up.

This is weird. Mom always opens the blinds first thing in the morning. Randy is up to something. She can only hope that he is out in town somewhere, buying car parts or beer, or meeting up with his friends who are even creepier than he is.

She tightens her towel around her waist and tiptoes forward, but as she turns toward the kitchen, she takes a sharp breath.

Randy.

Leaning against the wall next to the refrigerator, his arms crossed over his sunken chest. The flow from the air conditioning vent in the ceiling causes wisps of brown and gray hair to move around his balding head. The bottom of his saggy jeans covers half of his dirty bare feet. He's wearing a stained wife-beater, smeared with either engine grease or barbecue sauce. Please let it be grease, June thinks. At least that would mean he's been working on her car.

Randy's stink washes over her: an offensive mix of beer and bad life choices that barely covers the Drakkar he douses himself with on special occasions. She winces and braces herself for the tirade she knows is coming, but Randy just gives her an awkward smile, revealing his yellow teeth. Is he trying to be nice? Unlikely; he looks too much like a wild animal on the hunt.

Great, he's being a freak show again. She tries to ignore him and opens the refrigerator door. As she bends down to get a Coke from the bottom shelf, she gets a bad feeling in her gut.

He blows air between his teeth and sighs.

Oh god no. He's looking at my ass. Not again.

He's always been a lecherous creep, but since his attention turned to her about five months ago, being around him has been like walking through a minefield. For some reason, her mother turns a blind eye to his predatory behavior. When he started getting grabby, June pulled her mother aside and tried to get through to her, but Mom summarily dismissed everything June had to say. Now that she has to deal with him on her own, June feels like Bambi facing Godzilla.

"Don't you have something to do?" she asks, opening the Coke can with a loud pop.

"Oh!" Randy says with mock surprise. "Am I bothering you? In my own house? Looky looky, it's summer and here she is, *June in June*." He scratches his left armpit. "Yeah, I've got something to do. But listen up, you're still in trouble from last week, and I've been trying to think of a proper way to punish you. A way so you'll remember next time, for once."

June straightens her body and immediately tenses up. She doesn't know what he's talking about. What happened last week? They had a fight because she forgot to do the dishes and take out the garbage on Wednesday, but she didn't think it was that big of a deal.

Randy steps in closer. How can someone who never works out have such bad body odor? The stench makes her cough. He stares with wide eyes as the towel around her waist loosens.

After standing there for an eternity, he finally continues. "But then I thought, maybe it's time." It's subtle, but it's there, the slight slur in his words. He's hammered.

No, this is not going to end well.

"Time for what?" she says in a low voice, not wanting to hear the answer.

He leans in and whispers in her ear. "For punishment cock."

June's eyes burst open, and her jaw clenches so tightly she can hear her teeth grind. She turns her head to tell him to back off, but no words come out. Before she can take another breath, he reaches out and turns her chin with his hand and kisses her full on the lips. Vomit crawls up her throat; she swallows it back down, her vision blurring in a cloud of red. His face pulls back. Every ounce of her being wants to scream out, but she freezes, as if her body has turned to stone.

As he puts his arm around her waist and leans in again, June drops the Coke can, splashing soda on his jeans. He looks down at the mess and throws up his hands in disgust. "Goddamnit!"

With all her strength, June pushes him away. She spins around and runs outside into the glaring sunlight and sweltering heat, slamming the sliding glass door behind her.

After stumbling onto the grass by the pool, she falls down next to her sleeping friend, clutching her knees with her arms, sobbing.

Bree wakes up and asks groggily, "June? What's wrong? Did something happen?"

June continues rocking back and forth. Bree puts her arm around her and looks back at the house, confused and wondering: What is it this time? The sliding glass door answers with a simple reflection of the backyard, tree branches swaying in the light breeze. After a few minutes, the front door to the house bangs shut, followed by the thump of a heavy car door. The muscle car in the driveway roars to life, its tires screech down the street.

June looks up for a moment, then puts her head back down, crying harder, barely able to keep from choking.

Bree holds her friend tighter and whispers, "Oh, June."

An excerpt from the Introduction to *Vacaville: A History*
Sam Turnbill
Published 1988

The mythology of the American Dream persists with remarkable tenacity across generations. Its familiar elements—the white picket fence, two-car garage, and nuclear family—represent more than mere suburban aspirations; they constitute a foundational narrative that has shaped the nation's collective consciousness for decades. This idealized vision extends its influence throughout American culture, manifesting in everything from Hollywood productions to casual conversations among neighbors at the local grocery store.

Every historical era possesses its defining characteristics, and the post-war American Dream found its purest expression in the small towns scattered across the continent's vast interior. These communities, with their uncomplicated social structures and clearly defined values, served as living embodiments of the nation's most cherished ideals. Among such places, few exemplify this phenomenon more completely than a Northern California community that locals affectionately call "Cowtown"—a nickname derived both from its agricultural heritage and the literal Spanish translation of its official name.

Vacaville sits strategically positioned between San Francisco and Sacramento, occupying that distinctive space between urban sophistication and rural simplicity that characterizes much of California's Central Valley region. This single-high-school community presents all the expected elements of small-town America: pickup trucks with oversized tires, family-owned

establishments lining Main Street, and residential neighbor-
hoods filled with those archetypal two-car garages and nuclear
families.

The rhythms of community life follow predictable patterns. Each
spring, residents don their finest denim attire for the annual
pilgrimage to Andrews Park, where the Fiesta Days Parade cele-
brates the town's Spanish colonial heritage. Weekend editions of
the local newspaper invariably feature front-page coverage of
the high school football team's latest exploits. The community's
sole radio station, Quick 95.3 FM, provides a soundtrack of
contemporary soft rock, while the Mediterranean climate
ensures abundant sunshine and gentle breezes throughout most
of the year. To passing motorists on Interstate 80, Vacaville
appears as nothing more than a convenient rest stop, a place for
Californians to stop for gas or fast food on their way to
Sacramento.

This surface tranquility, however, conceals a more complex
reality that becomes apparent to anyone observing the community's younger residents. With limited entertainment options
available, there is little for teenagers to do but get into trouble.
High school athletes navigate the streets in their pickup trucks
after practice, shouting provocations and crude assessments of
any young men who happen to cross their paths. Downtown
establishments like Exodus Mart serve as unofficial gathering
points for various youth subcultures, where teenagers congre-
gate on weekend evenings, skating against curbs and railings,
smoking clove cigarettes and maintaining vigilant watch for
approaching police cruisers that might round the corner onto
Main Street. The local Dollar Theater serves as another focal
point for teenage social life, though the outdated films it screens
often reinforce rather than alleviate the sense of cultural isola-
tion experienced by many young residents.

These characteristics could describe countless American communities from Ohio to Nebraska, from Texas to Montana. Vacaville's devotion to high school athletics, its agricultural roots, and its small-town social dynamics place it firmly within the mainstream of American suburban experience. Yet one crucial factor distinguishes this community from its countless counterparts across the nation: its proximity to one of California's most significant correctional institutions.

Standing against the foothills on the south side of town is California State Prison, Solano—Vacaville's only claim to fame. That it operates as a medium-security facility offers little consolation to the residents living in its shadow. Current overcrowding has only intensified their concerns, adding an element of complexity to what might otherwise appear as another unremarkable suburban community.

2

GOUGE AWAY

THROWING BACK THE COVERS, June rises on Monday, her mind set on finding answers. There must be an explanation. Sure, Randy is a douchebag, but it can't be as bad as she thinks. Because that would be crazy, right?

He couldn't have said that yesterday. And whatever happened, he was just drunk again. It's not the first time his drinking has caused problems, but she wasn't ready for it this time. That must be it. Maybe if she could talk to him, as much as she hates seeing his ugly face, he'd admit it was all a mistake— or maybe he wouldn't even remember doing it. She doesn't know which would be worse. Either way, this isn't the kind of thing she can sweep under the rug.

After brushing her hair in the mirror on her dresser, she opens her underwear drawer, reaches into the back, and pulls out a large white tube sock stuffed with all kinds of bills. She holds it up and admires its weight, then puts it back and closes the drawer. It's enough to know it's there.

The hoard of money began after her father died when she was sixteen. He didn't have much, but he left her $2,500 in his will. Her mother didn't trust June, so she made her open a joint bank account with both of their names on it. And June didn't trust her mother either, so over the months and years, she periodically took out small amounts of cash from the ATM near school and slipped it into her sacred white sock in her underwear drawer after she came home. Since her mother never washed June's laundry—or did anything for June, for that matter —the dresser drawer seemed as safe a place as any. She added to her stash when she started her restaurant job.

It is her emergency fund, perhaps unnecessary, though it helps her anxiety to know that she is prepared for anything.

June trudges downstairs and drops her backpack on the kitchen table. The sound of running water upstairs tells her that her mother is in the shower. Then it happens.

A loud clang, coming from the garage.

Randy.

June closes her eyes and says to herself: Just do it, let's get this over with so we can all move on. The door to the garage creaks as she pokes her head inside.

Her VW Bug is parked on blocks in front of her. The left side of the garage is empty except for a sheet of aluminum on the floor, covered with large streaks of oil. And there he is, in all his disgusting glory, getting some tools from the counter on the far right side. Tinkering with cars is all he does when he's not on a business trip, when he's not drinking beer and watching his precious new television. He tinkers, but never seems to get anything done.

She steps in quietly, feeling like a rabbit sneaking into a deep, dark cave where a hungry bear is hibernating. He turns and notices her, then goes back to cleaning his tools with a dirty rag.

"Hey, June, morning. Off to school?"

"In a minute, mom's still getting ready." Weird, he's acting like nothing happened. Maybe he really doesn't remember? The hairs on the back of her neck stand up. She forces herself to walk further into the garage, up to the headlights of her car. The realization that the best she can hope for is that he's just a bad drunk makes her start to shake. The impulse to suddenly run away shoots through her, but no, she has to press on, to be certain.

She casually asks him how things are going with her car. When he gives her some inane excuse, like he always does, she asks why it's taking so long.

"You've got a one-track mind," he says, with deliberate hostility, throwing his rag on the counter. "Ungrateful kid."

"Um," she says, ignoring his vitriol, desperately trying to be firm, "we need to talk."

"About what?"

"About what happened yesterday." Unable to meet his glare, she looks down at the aluminum sheet on the floor.

"What happened yesterday?" he asks, wiping his brow with the back of his hand. He grabs a wrench from his toolbox on the counter, then nods his head in recognition. "Oh, that… right." He drops the wrench onto the table with a loud clank, picks up a towel, and slowly wipes his greasy hands, a slight smirk lifting the corners of his crooked mouth.

"I know. It was a mistake," June says, leading him on. This is where you apologize, she thinks. I'll be good. I'll try not to make this too awkward for you. I'll be off to school in a few minutes, and maybe we can all get back to some kind of normalcy around here.

"No, June, that was no mistake." Randy waits for her to look up and stares into her eyes, still slowly wiping his hands.

It feels as if her clothes have suddenly burst into flames. She crosses her arms over her chest and looks away, focusing on the small opaque windows in the closed garage door. If someone were outside, they couldn't see in; she wonders if they would hear her if she screamed.

He continues in a low, deliberate voice. "I've wanted you for a long time, ever since me and your mom got together."

June's heart stops. Her breath comes in short gasps—like she is swimming and going under. She turns her head, trying to hide her distress as best as she can. Almost to herself, she says weakly, "Does mom know?"

Randy drops his towel on the floor and takes a step closer.

June crawls out of her skin. No, don't come near me. She closes her eyes and feels the room spin around her.

Randy continues, every sound of his voice clawing at her ears, deep enough to scar. "I've waited as long as I could. It's about time now, girl."

"Please stop talking," June whispers.

He takes another step. "Oh, I'm not going to stop. I'm not going to stop a goddamn thing." He leans in close, speaking low near her ear. "No mistake, this is going to happen."

Her body goes numb as the veil of any illusion of working this out is violently torn away. Reeling, she has to reach out and put her hand on the hood of her car to keep from falling over. This can't be happening. He can't have just said that. A tear runs down her left cheek.

He's still close to her face, and though his voice is low, it sounds like the thunder that precedes a tornado. "And don't even think about telling your mother. Or anyone. Don't make this worse for yourself, girl. Besides, who do you think they would believe? I'll try not to make this hurt unless I have to."

June closes her eyes as the panic sets in, mouthing the words to herself: *It already hurts.*

She bites her lip—deep enough to bleed. Just to feel the pain, to keep herself from screaming.

The kitchen door creaks open; her mother pops her head into the garage. "June, where are y—? Oh, there you are. It's time to go. Got to get you to school if I'm going to make it to work on time. We're running late as it is."

June pushes past her and hurries down the hall. Her mother

stands there with her mouth open. "June? What happened to your lip?"

"Nothing, I'm fine," June calls back over her shoulder, trying to keep her voice from shaking. "Can we just go?"

Her mother gives Randy a worried, questioning look.

He shrugs his shoulders. "Kids these days…"

3

TALK ABOUT THE PASSION

THE THIRD-PERIOD BELL rang over twenty minutes ago, but you wouldn't know it from the way the kids are acting. Robert Sampson sighs and makes a mental note to rethink his career choices tonight over a bottle of Pinot Noir. Every year he wishes the local community college would have an opening, but their history department is full of lifers who will never retire or move away. He will just have to wait for one of them to die. Sampson raises his voice in a vain attempt to regain control of the class.

"Once again, it's the 12th and 13th centuries, and we're in the steppe plateau of Central Asia. The Mongol tribe has really gone on the rampage, causing a lot of death and destruction, as expected. All led by our good friend, Genghis Khan. Now, I'm sure you've heard the old trope in fiction, the one that asks: What would have happened if someone had gone back in time and assassinated Hitler before World War II? Well, let's apply that idea here. So my question to you now is: How many people might have survived if somebody had assassinated Mr. Khan before he rose to full power?"

No reaction, although the class is anything but silent. At least they're still in their seats. That's Sampson's real goal: to keep their butts in their seats and survive this week. He always loathes the last week of school with a passion reserved for the particularly abhorrent—like drunk drivers, child molesters, and big hairy spiders—and this year is no different.

This is not the Honors U.S. History class; they meet down the hall with Mrs. Stein. Sampson harbors a deep-seated resentment toward her and her smug attitude, as well as her spacious classroom with huge windows along the entire left side.

No, this is just good old normal core U.S. History, which takes place in the last room on the right side of Building C—one of the smallest rooms on campus. There are two tiny windows on the right wall, one of them covered with cardboard after someone vandalized the room three months ago.

At least this isn't Credit Recovery U.S. History, where students who have previously failed the course try to get the credits they need to graduate. Sampson always told himself if they assigned him to that class, he would simply turn in his keys, drive away, and never look back.

He rolls up the sleeves of his white dress shirt and calls out, "Anyone?"

A male voice in the back of the class says, "Anyone... anyone? Bueller?" Laughter fills the room.

Sampson's glare shoots daggers into the back row.

Jake Meers.

Little shit. Sampson smiles to himself, knowing that Mr. Meers will indeed be taking the Credit Recovery version of this class next year. Or over the summer, if he wants to be eligible for football in the fall. Sampson knows he could rip Jake a new one right now, but he lets it go. The time to assert his authority over these mouth breathers is long gone. He keeps reminding himself: Focus. Just get through this week.

He looks around at the forty-three kids in his least favorite class, most of them only half-awake, with stupid looks on their pale, fat faces. Is this the generation that will inherit the world someday? Lord, help us all.

He stubbornly sticks to his original lesson plan: to lecture all week and give the kids an experience they will never forget. The concept is simple. Cover a different major era and region each day as a preview of what they will all face in World History next year—well, all of them except for the not-so-wide receiver Jake Meers.

Too many teachers check out and give up along with the kids at the end of the year. They show movies or play silly little games like Hangman or History Jeopardy. In his fourth year at this less-than-prestigious institution in the middle of Cowtown, he wants to actually teach something this week. That's what they pay him for, and that's what he's going to deliver.

Of course, he may have bitten off more than he can chew. It's a struggle to keep the kids in the classroom at all, let alone in their seats. Usually during the last week of school, the kids get up and mill around the door for the last ten minutes of class; some of them inevitably spill out into the hallway and wander away, prompting Principal McCallister to call Sampson back into his office for a good reaming. Last year, despite his verbal warnings, Sampson had to physically stand in front of the door to keep the kids from leaving.

This time, he knows he's got to try something different, something that truly packs a punch. Because the kids' collective attention spans are so limited, he has decided to approach the last week of school with more visceral material than the curriculum would normally allow. It's risky, but so what? He has to do whatever it takes to keep the kids in line for the fifty-five minutes he is stuck with them. If Principal McCallister gives him any trouble, Sampson will simply remind him that with forty-five kids in this small room, he is way over the fire code and should have notified the teachers union by now.

He raises his voice again, not bothering to hide his annoyance. "Seriously? People, I just told you. We just went over this a few minutes ago." There must be at least one of them paying attention. But even that four-eyed Todd Stansfield in the front row looks away as he keeps touching the pimple on his chin.

Sarah Parsley raises her hand.

Sampson arches an eyebrow. This could go either way. Sarah is an average student, but she's also a total suck-up. Maybe she just wants attention.

"Sarah? How many?" He asks, approaching her desk. "How many people would have survived on the steppe plateau of Central Asia if Genghis Khan had not been around?"

"A hundred thousand?" Sarah says, raising her voice at the end and hunching her shoulders.

"No, Sarah, but thanks for trying." Sampson returns to his podium as giggles erupt from the back of the class. He continues, "No, more like somewhere between *twenty and fifty million people*."

Although there are whispers in the back row, the front of the class is silent; some kids are even sitting up straight. Eager to build on this new momentum, Sampson presses on. "That's right, under our friend Mr. Khan, the Mongols ruled with an iron fist. No one was safe. The enemy tribes of the steppe had only two choices: surrender or be destroyed. But surrender was its own nightmare."

The kids in the back jerk their heads up. This is the quietest the class has been all morning.

"You're not going to learn about this next year, but I'll dial you in. For now, think about it. What could that have been? Why would surrender seem almost as bad as dying? What could the Mongols have done that would be so brutal?

He looks around the room. Some kids look confused, some have raised eyebrows, but one in the second row is just staring off into space.

June Addison.

She never fit in. Her green eyes are a little too big for her face, which is always washed out because she never seems to wear any makeup to school. Recently, for some reason, she dyed her hair red—a nice change, but now it's tied back in a ponytail with little strands leaking out here and there. She's wearing a black Bad Religion t-shirt and faded blue jeans, with black and white Chuck Taylors that might have been new a few years ago. All the other girls in school cake on so much makeup, and the way they dress, you would think they were going out to a dance club instead of going to class. To him, it's like June just doesn't care. Sampson keeps wondering why she doesn't just take the GED and get out of this place.

He railed against her being added to his class, but to no avail. The memory sticks in his mind like a broken record left on in a back room, skipping over and over, never getting to the good part of the song.

It was a Wednesday afternoon in September, during Sampson's prep period. Principal McCallister had called him into his office for a special meeting. Sampson sat in front of his boss in the chair usually reserved for the parents of problem kids, with Lucy Waller (the assistant principal) next to him. His boss had a worried look on his face, as if he didn't know where to begin.

"Bob," he said, "I know you're wondering why we called you in here. This is about your third-period history class."

Sampson was immediately annoyed. What could this possibly be about? They can't add another kid to third period; the class limit is thirty-five, and they've already added four more kids since school started two weeks ago. Some years, it seems like they add students all year long.

His boss took a deep breath, looked down, and got right into it. "We're adding another student to your class. She starts tomorrow."

Shit.

It took all of Sampson's energy not to say the word out loud.

"We just want to go over a few things with you first."

Sampson's head started throbbing. This was highly unusual. They'd never had meetings about adding kids to a class before. New students always showed up with add cards in their hands, and you just had to deal with it. This is not going to end well.

He tried not to raise his voice, but he had to say something. "No way, we're at thirty-nine kids in that class. That's already over the limit, and that room is way too small."

Principal McCallister folded his hands on his desk in front of him and flashed a condescending little smile. "I get it. But you know the rules: we have to give every transfer student the same class they had from wherever they came from, or an equivalent. I'm sorry, Bob, but our hands are tied."

"Fine." Sampson knew the rule was bullshit, but he also knew it was futile to fight the system. "Then why am I here?"

His boss sighed. "This one has a... little history of her own."

Sampson couldn't believe it. What now? He said in a weak voice, "Uh, excuse me?"

It was Lucy Waller's turn to chime in. "Look, she's had a hard time. She just needs a little help and understanding."

Sampson ran a hand through his thinning brown hair and began laying bricks and mortar in his mind, walling off his emotions. He said nothing, just stared at the floor.

Lucy opened a folder on her lap and ran her index finger down a list on the first page. She continued in a voice too perky for the moment. "Her dad died in '85 when she was a sophomore. Car accident, terrible tragedy. She was in the car, too—survived with only some cuts and bruises, as far as we know. She took it so hard she dropped out of school, got into some trouble. The next year she went to Country High. You know, where the delinquents go. But she seems like a good kid. She didn't last four months there. Frankly, I don't blame her."

"I still don't understand why she's in my class now," Sampson said.

She closed the folder. "Her mother was supposed to be home-schooling her, but you know how these things go. At least the kid was sharp enough to test out of her sophomore term. Now her mother wants her to do her junior year here. Of course, because of her age, we said no."

Principal McCallister leaned back in his chair. "But they played hardball."

"Wait, how old is she now?" Sampson asked, his mind racing. "She's what, eighteen now?" His boss was an ex-Marine who ran a tight ship and was always in control. How did they strong-arm this guy? Then it came to him: football. In a small town like this, it always comes back to the high school football team—which brings us to the other thing we never talk about at this school. "Man alive, does Bobby Thompson still go here?"

Bobby Thompson—the ringer. He is at least twenty years old, a three-year senior. He never graduates, just keeps taking easy gym classes every semester and continues to dominate at defensive tackle. And no one ever said anything about it, at least not until June Addison's mother showed up.

Sampson's eyes narrowed as he pieced it together. "Oh, I see," he said, each syllable dripping with suspicion. "So her mom said something like, 'If you want to make State this year, you'll let my little girl come back like nothing happened.' Is that it?"

Principal McCallister opened his mouth in a knowing smile. "Like I said, Bob, our hands are tied."

So here she is at the end of the year, nineteen years old now, sitting in his class against his better judgment. Sampson was worried at first; he smelled trouble on her. There was no way a high school kid that age wouldn't have an attitude problem a mile wide. But to her credit, she never stood out. She was almost invisible, kept to herself and maintained her C average all year long. Probably did the same in all of her classes.

Here is a kid the same age as most of the students he would be teaching if he ever secured that community college position he's been dreaming of. Sampson bets they would care more about their education than these kids. Could June give him a glimpse of what that would be like? Could she, even now, put forth more than a mediocre effort? Come on kid, it's the last week of school. This is your last chance. Show me what you've got.

Sampson beams at the class and continues. "So, the Mongols would sack a town, then go around asking everyone about their skills. Anyone who was useful got put to work—that's how they survived. As for everyone and everything else? The Mongols killed or destroyed it all. Simple as that. But there was one other way to make it through more or less intact. Anyone know what that might have been?"

No one answers, but at least the class is quiet now.

Sampson raises his voice as he goes into detail. "Concubines. The Mongols had this practice of taking women as concubines. Wives, essentially. Taken women, spoils of war—call it what you will. But not marriage as you or I think of it. A coerced union, a forced marriage... that doesn't sound very consensual to me. Many would say it's akin to violation. It sounds like we're talking about rape, right? That sounds a lot like rape. And yet history books always refer to these women as wives."

His eyes wander, lost in thought. "The Mongols weren't alone. Their sprees of violence and rape mirror the actions of many conquerors throughout history. The Romans and the

Greeks included. But the Mongols? They were extreme, even by those standards. They took it to another level. Maybe they raped so much because of their constant success in battle. They kept winning, so they kept raping. Not a good time for anyone living in the steppe plateau."

He chuckles to himself. "I guess you could say there were a lot of *steppe* dads."

No one gets the joke. The class sits in awkward silence. Outside in the nearby parking lot, a car alarm squeaks, a door slams, an engine revs.

"But here's where it gets interesting. Think about it. What was their real motivation for these heinous acts? Were they simply enjoying their conquests? Taking pleasure in plunder, if you will. Or was it something else? Were they tormenting those tribes for standing up to them?"

He tilts his head and scans the class. Nothing but vacant looks. Moving closer, he stands in front of June's desk. She's lost, with a thousand-yard stare.

"June, what do you think? Did the Mongols get off on it, or was this some kind of punishment?"

She finally raises her head, though the faraway look in her eyes doesn't fade. Her lips part but no words come out. Looking away, she stares off into space again and quickly wipes her eyes with her sleeve.

Sampson has to admit it; he resents her. They forced him to take her into this class. In fact, he resents all these kids. All of them with their vapid, empty looks. And this one, this spoiled little girl, just waiting for school to end, not taking advantage of her position in life. Sampson wishes he could be nineteen again. Oh, the things he would do.

"Were you even paying attention?" he asks, yelling now. "All of you precious little ones with your everybody-gets-a-medal moments. You act like it's always been this way. You have no idea how hard people have worked for you to have what you have. The sacrifices they made. And it's all wasted on you! I know it's the last week of school, but we still have some time left. And it's *my time*. You're not free of me yet. You could all show a little respect. A little common courtesy. And you, June, you'll never amount to anything if you don't apply yourself."

He goes back to the front of the class and shouts, "People, can you all just apply yourselves? Take some initiative. Can you do that for once in your lives? Maybe we need a little *punishment* around here. Maybe then you'll all listen, for once."

June grabs her purse and backpack and runs out of the classroom, the door swinging behind her. No one says a word.

Sampson throws his hands up and says, "What did I say?!"

Screw it, he thinks, it's not worth the effort. Tomorrow, I'm showing a movie.

From *Vacaville: A History*
Sam Turnbill
Published 1988

While many consider the prison complex Vacaville's primary claim to fame, local residents increasingly view it as more of a curse than a blessing. Recent tough-on-crime legislation has created severe overcrowding throughout California's correctional system, and Vacaville bears a disproportionate share of this crisis. The installation of double and triple bunk beds in cells designed for single occupancy makes the problem impossible to ignore, as the facility now houses one of the largest inmate populations in the nation. Yet residents worry about more than the impact of continued prison expansion on local property values. Their deeper concerns center on the adjacent medical facility and the disturbing rumors surrounding its treatment of the inmates.

The medical complex predates the main prison by decades. California Medical Facility opened in 1955, officially designated to care for elderly, disabled, and seriously ill inmates from across the state's male prison population. While it serves as the flagship of California's correctional healthcare system, CMF has gained notoriety primarily through its roster of infamous inmates.

Among the facility's more notable residents was counterculture figure Timothy Leary, who served time there from 1973 to 1974 for marijuana possession and escape from a minimum-security facility in San Luis Obispo. Compared to many of CMF's other occupants, Leary represented the gentler end of the criminal spectrum. The majority of inmates housed there had committed far more violent offenses.

Edmund Kemper, known as the "Co-ed Killer," arrived at CMF in late 1973 under a life sentence for a series of brutal murders. His criminal history began early: at fifteen, he killed his grandparents in cold blood. Nine years later, he embarked on a killing spree in the Santa Cruz area, murdering and dismembering six female hitchhikers. He concluded his rampage by killing his mother and one of her friends before voluntarily surrendering to authorities.

The facility also housed Theodore Streleski, a Stanford mathematics graduate student who murdered his faculty advisor with a sledgehammer in 1978. After nineteen years as a doctoral candidate while supporting himself through various jobs, Streleski claimed his crime was justified, citing his advisor's alleged denial of awards, public humiliation, and refusal of financial assistance. The court rejected his defense, sentencing him to seven years at Vacaville.

Gregory Powell, one of the notorious Onion Field killers, also served time at CMF following his conviction for murdering a Los Angeles police officer in 1963. Powell and his accomplice Jimmy Lee Smith kidnapped two plainclothes Hollywood officers during a traffic stop, transporting them to an onion field near Bakersfield where they executed one of the officers. The case became a landmark in American criminal justice, inspiring both an acclaimed true crime book and film while forcing the LAPD and other major departments to completely revise their field procedures and tactical approaches.

Perhaps the most infamous resident in CMF's history was Charles Manson, who was incarcerated there on two separate occasions: briefly in 1974, then for nine years beginning in May 1976. During his Vacaville tenure, Manson granted his first major interview in 1981 to Tom Snyder for NBC's late-night program *Tomorrow Coast to Coast*, displaying the same bizarre speaking style and twisted worldview that had characterized his criminal career.

Manson had been convicted of conspiracy to commit murder for orchestrating several killings carried out by his followers, known as the Manson Family. This commune-like group had emerged in the California desert during the late 1960s, with all the murders committed by members acting under Manson's direct orders. He believed these killings would trigger an apocalyptic race war he called "Helter Skelter."

Surprisingly, Manson also pursued musical interests while incarcerated. Between 1983 and 1984, he collaborated with fellow inmate Eddie Ragsdale, known as "Rags," to compose and record more than ten cassette tapes of original music. These recordings vanished for many years under mysterious circumstances before eventually being recovered and released as a vinyl album titled "The Lost Vacaville Tapes."

4

MAD WORLD

LATER THAT NIGHT, June walks around the house in a daze. She avoids interacting with anyone, but it's not like they notice—her mother and Creepy Randy are too busy arguing about credit card bills and what should be next on the house fix-it list.

Dinner is torture. It takes all of her energy to sit at the table when every part of her wants to run upstairs and scream into her pillow. Being around Randy makes her skin crawl. Every time he speaks, it feels like someone is hitting the side of her head with a hammer. She can't look him in the face; whenever he addresses her, she stares blankly at her mother, who keeps her eyes on her plate while cutting her chicken into smaller and smaller pieces.

Later, after a lull in the conversation, her mother finally looks at June and says, "Honey, are you all right? You've barely touched your food."

"I'm not five, Mom."

Her mother makes a face. "You need to eat."

"Actually, I feel sick. Can I be excused?"

"Fine, go to your room. I'll do the dishes. *Again*."

June sees spots on her way up the stairs and almost falls over. Once in her room, she closes the door behind her and paces back and forth, carefully avoiding the squeaky floorboards on the right side near the window. It's killing her, but she can't put this off any longer. She has to talk to her mother and tell her what happened with Randy.

She always knew this was going to be a problem, but she put off dealing with it because there was no way of knowing how her mother would react. It's not subtle. Randy is disgusting. He constantly leers at every girl with two legs and a pulse, regardless of age. Yet somehow, her mother remains oblivious. For her own sake, June tries to ignore him to keep the peace. But ignoring a problem doesn't make it go away, and some things just get worse with time.

June keeps pacing, trying to stave off the panic attack she knows is coming. Though she is strong in her resolve, that doesn't make this mess any easier to deal with.

She stops and listens, the familiar sounds at the end of dinner causing a pain in her chest: dishes clinking together, water running in the sink.

They're done eating. Now Randy will do what he always does—sit in front of his big TV, drink beer, and watch Monday Night Bullshit or whatever sports show is on this month.

Footsteps thump up the stairs; the third step groans in defiance. Her mother, no doubt. She's going into her room, doing her nightly routine. Though her mood swings are a mystery, her habits and behavior are always predictable.

June waits a few minutes, then quietly crosses the hall to her mother's bedroom. She's lying on her bed, reading *Cosmo,* with purple goo all over her face. June sits down on the bed near her mother's feet and looks at the floor.

Her mother flips through the pages. "Hey, did you know there are fifteen ways to make your breasts look bigger?"

"Mom, we need to talk."

"Okay, honey." She puts the magazine down against her chest. "Are you sick? Should I take your temperature?"

"No." June takes a deep breath.

"What is it this time?" Her mother looks at June, waiting for an answer, until her expression suddenly changes and she gasps. "Oh my god, are you pregnant?"

"What? No... no," June says, shaking her head. She puts her hands to her face and starts crying. "I don't know how to say this..."

It doesn't take long for June to get an icy feeling in her gut. She doesn't know what she's expecting, but it's not this. Maybe it's the way her mother stiffens up as soon as June starts recounting the events of the previous afternoon. Maybe it's the way her mother holds her breath, takes too long to respond, as if she needs to think it all through—as if she has to consider all of her options about what to do next.

At least her mother is patient; she lets June finish her story. After a few moments of silence, she places her hand on June's knee.

"That doesn't sound like Randy."

"Come on, Mom, wake up, look who we're talking about. It sounds *a lot* like Randy." June struggles to keep her voice down; she doesn't want him to overhear her. She needs her mother on her side before this whole situation blows up, as it inevitably will. They need to present a united front before he gets the chance to abuse them both when his rage boils over.

"If there's anything I've learned," her mother says, and something in her tone makes June's heart sink, "it's that there are two sides to every story. It wouldn't be fair if I didn't hear his side of all this."

June's jaw drops. "God, Mom, how can you take his side?"

"I'm not taking sides, honey. I just want to talk to him. Look around, look at all this." She waves her arm in front of her, at the room and its furnishings. "He works so hard, does so well for himself, and he takes good care of us. I owe it to him to at least hear him out."

No, June thinks, you owe it to me to take care of me and keep me safe.

She mutters under her breath, barely getting the words out, "He said he's always wanted me. From the beginning. He's practically a child molester."

Her mother gives June a blank look and says matter-of-factly, "You're over eighteen."

June knows the real saying: There are three sides to every story—yours, mine, and the truth. She also knows that even if she is only half-right, this whole situation is all kinds of wrong. The main point, now painfully obvious, is that June is not safe here. It's that simple. If her mother doesn't come to her senses soon, June doesn't know what she will have to do.

5

YOUR PRETTY FACE IS GOING TO HELL

JUNE WAITED in her room until she heard her mother's footsteps going downstairs, then snuck back to the stairs and sat on the top step. She couldn't see anything, but wanted to hear as much as possible.

Her mother began speaking in hushed tones. June couldn't hear Randy's answers, but they were short, and her mother raised her voice in response. Here come the fireworks, June thought.

"But she's my daughter!"

"God christ! What is it with you, Gail? You always have to push my buttons. Maybe it's time I pushed back."

Heavy footsteps echoed across the living room floor. June imagined Randy getting out of his chair, his beer gut jutting out comically as he tried to assert himself.

"You wouldn't dare," Gail said, backing away.

June whispered to herself, "You better not hurt her."

"Try me." Randy threw the TV remote down, bouncing it off the coffee table.

Gail crossed her arms over her chest. "I think you should leave."

"You want me to go? Oh, I'll go!"

A crash rang out. He threw his beer bottle at the wall. Shattering glass, splashing liquid—just like on MTV. June was afraid the neighbors would call the police.

"See how you do without me." The front door slammed behind him. Gail put her hands over her face and sobbed. A car started outside and roared down the street into the night.

Of course, none of that happened.

What do you want to be when you grow up?

It's a question June struggles with as much as anyone. How do you make lasting change? Does the caterpillar molt into its shiny chrysalis with intention and purpose, or is it mindless, simply nature's design? At nineteen, June still feels so young. She never had the chance to grow up. Awkward, stunted, forever destined to be the ugly duckling. Her days are things to be endured; it's a struggle to survive, let alone try to seem like a normal person. She doesn't blame herself, not for all of it. She can't imagine her home life is something that could ever be considered normal.

No, what's really happening tonight is not so exciting, so dramatic, so ready for prime time.

Randy is at the refrigerator, beer bottles clinking together as he grabs another one from the box on the bottom shelf. Like most nights when he is at home and on a tear, there will be a lot of clinking bottles tonight. His La-Z-Boy recliner squeaks as he settles his fat ass back down.

"Hey Gail, what's up?"

"We need to talk."

"Damn, what now? Can't this wait until after the game?"

June strains to hear, but Gail speaks too low; she can only make out Randy's side of the conversation. At first he feigns indignation. She should have known he would deny everything. June hadn't really expected anything less. But her mother will have her back, will put her foot down at last. Maybe we can have some sense in this house for once. June feels a surge of anticipation. It's happening, it's all finally happening. When everything is out in the open—what then? Will her mother leave him? If there's any sense in this universe, she will.

"It's weird," Randy says, sounding confused. "Don't be mad at her. I think she's always had eyes for me. It's kind of sad, really."

June can't breathe. Scorching thoughts machine-gun fire through her addled brain. What? Now he's blaming me? You sad, pathetic piece of shit, like I would ever come on to you. I would rather stick my hand in a bag of tarantulas.

Randy takes a soothing tone, and they both lower their voices. June keeps leaning forward, but it's no use; there's no way to make any sense of the undertones. She cautiously moves down another step on the staircase. This is all wrong. This isn't how it's supposed to be. Where are mom's cries of righteous anger? Why isn't Randy yelling at her and threatening to kick us both out? Where is his "I'll do what I want, don't tell me what to do" speech? June puts her hand to her stomach, afraid she'll lose what little dinner she ate all over the stairs. A little voice in her head says: *This will not end well.*

Bottles clink in the recycling bin in the pantry. Footsteps move toward the stairs.

June hastens back to her room and sits on her bed. Staring off into space, she picks at her fingers, making her right thumb bleed. She can't believe it. This can't be happening. Not Mom. No, not her. June didn't expect this, because this wasn't in the realm of possibility. Sure, her mother can be a narcissistic bitch who sometimes forgets June exists—but no one would let this happen to their own daughter. What kind of monster would do that?

A light knock on the door. Gail stands in the doorway.

"Can I come in?"

"Okay," June mumbles without looking up.

Gail sits down on the bed next to June and strokes her hair. June can't feel it; her whole body is numb. She closes her eyes as Gail talks, explaining Randy's denial, saying things that mean nothing to June. Useless words that only make a bigger mess of things. June's life is over. Where do we go from here?

Then Gail becomes authoritative, the harsh words grinding together in June's mind. She might as well be standing in the middle of a steel mill.

"I've got a lot on my plate these days, June. You know that. I could use your help. And with all my hours at work now, you'll actually be spending a lot more time with Randy." She puts her hand on June's leg. June has the sudden urge to set her mother on fire.

"I need you to be a team player here. I know it's been tough with your dad gone, but Randy, he's a good guy... I think you just never gave him a chance. I wish you could see what I see."

June scrunches her face, forcing herself not to shout out the questions that are exploding through her: Are you fucking blind? So what if he has a nice house? What is the color of the sky in *your* world?

To avoid a slap, June keeps her face blank, but the thoughts keep swirling. What power does he have over you? You're willing to sell me out for mere convenience, what is wrong with you?

She says, "But I'm your daughter. Why don't I come first? Don't I even register with you anymore?"

June knows the answer—they both fell apart after June's father died. It happened in the winter, just after June had turned sixteen. Gail simply receded into a ball of nothingness. June had to learn to take care of herself, but basic survival was all she could handle. It wasn't long before she stopped going to school altogether. Gail didn't notice until truancy officers came to the door and gave them ultimatums they both ignored. School turned out to be the least of their worries. They lost the house and had to move into a cramped apartment on the south side of town. Until later, when Randy showed up and everything changed overnight.

Although Gail seems unaware of how disgusting Randy is, she doesn't have a blind spot for his money. It's the gleam in her eye. She's been with me my whole life, June thinks, but I don't know her at all. June always feared her mother was only with Randy for the money and lifestyle he could give her. Regardless, that is Gail's choice; June shouldn't have to be the one to pay the price.

"Of course you register, honey," Gail says. "Honestly, I don't know where you get this stuff. I think you need some rest, you've got school tomorrow. And remember, team player, right?"

June nods and lets her hair fall down to cover her face. She blinks, tears running down her cheeks. Gail doesn't notice; she is already leaving the room, closing the door behind her.

Why won't she stand up to him? Can't she see what's going on? June falls down on her bed and sobs into her pillow.

Do you really think he won't try to touch me as soon as your back is turned?

No, this won't end well. Something terrible is going to happen, and the way Randy has been leering at her lately, it won't be long. He's always been a bad drunk, and whenever he drinks, bad things happen. Just because nobody else notices doesn't make it right. And it's not like they can talk it out. She already tried that, and he turned it around on her. Mom is perhaps the worst of all, willing to sell out her own daughter for the few comforts of her stupid little life.

Too many things come too easily for most people, like keeping the status quo and not rocking the boat. Well, this boat needs to be rocked. It needs to be blown right out of the water.

What do I want to be when I grow up? Not violated. Growing up means taking action, real action—not just doing things because you're supposed to, or going through the motions like you always have. It means doing the right thing, even if it goes against your own comfort.

Growing up means doing what you must, even if it terrifies you.

June sits up and leans forward, puts her arms around her knees, and closes her eyes.

If no one will take care of this, I'll do it myself.

I'll do what I have to do.

I'll just have to kill him.

From *Vacaville: A History*
Sam Turnbill
Published 1988

California Medical Facility stands as more than just another state prison—it serves as the cornerstone of California's correctional healthcare system. Since its establishment, CMF has pioneered numerous innovative programs addressing the complex medical and psychological needs of inmates throughout the region. Among its notable initiatives was the Blind Project, launched in the 1960s, which trained inmates to produce Braille transcriptions and audio recordings of books. The facility also gained recognition for treating the state prison system's first AIDS patient, subsequently developing specialized treatment protocols that would be implemented across other institutions.

Yet beneath these humanitarian achievements lurked persistent questions about the quality of care being provided. By the late 1980s, serious concerns had reached the highest levels of government. In 1987, the U.S. Department of Justice formally notified Governor George Deukmejian about troubling deficiencies in the facility's ability to adequately treat inmates with severe medical conditions. The following year brought a damning lawsuit that characterized CMF as a "filthy, vermin-infested, overcrowded prison" where medical treatment fell far below acceptable standards. The irony was stark: overcrowding had apparently undermined the very programs the facility had pioneered, including AIDS treatment.

However, the most disturbing allegations surrounding Vacaville emerge not from official reports, but from the shadowy world of government conspiracy and covert operations.

For decades during the Cold War era, the Central Intelligence Agency operated an illegal research program known as Project MKUltra. This clandestine initiative sought to develop sophisticated techniques for controlling human behavior and extracting information from unwilling subjects. The experiments, conducted on both voluntary and involuntary participants, frequently involved the administration of powerful hallucinogenic drugs. The ultimate goal was to create methods for breaking down an individual's psychological defenses, making them more susceptible to interrogation and manipulation.

The full scope of MKUltra remained hidden until 1977, when Senate investigations triggered by Freedom of Information Act requests uncovered approximately 20,000 classified documents. Even today, many records remain sealed, their contents known only to a select few within the intelligence community.

According to conspiracy researchers, Vacaville's medical facility served as one of the primary testing sites for these disturbing experiments. They allege that inmates—many of whom never consented to participate—were subjected to horrific procedures under CIA supervision. One particularly brutal technique, known as anectine therapy, involved injecting subjects with a drug that temporarily paralyzed their breathing muscles. As victims experienced the terror of suffocation, technicians would threaten them with death unless they cooperated with interrogators. Only then would they activate life support equipment to revive the subject.

The case of Donald Cinque DeFreeze adds another layer to these conspiracy theories.

DeFreeze's early life followed a familiar pattern of petty crime and police cooperation. During the 1960s, he worked as an informant for the Los Angeles Police Department while building a criminal record of his own. From 1969 to 1972, he served time at Vacaville for armed robbery—a period that coincided precisely with the CIA's documented presence at the adjacent medical facility.

After his release, DeFreeze transformed into something far more dangerous. He founded the Symbionese Liberation Army, a radical terrorist organization that would soon capture national attention through one of the most sensational crimes of the decade. In February 1974, the SLA kidnapped newspaper heiress Patty Hearst from her Berkeley apartment, subsequently using psychological manipulation techniques to convert her into an active participant in their criminal activities. The case dominated headlines for months and raised troubling questions about the nature of psychological control.

Conspiracy theorists argue that DeFreeze's transformation was no coincidence. They suggest that his time at Vacaville served as a testing ground for mind control techniques, and that the Hearst kidnapping represented a real-world application of CIA research. In this interpretation, the entire episode was orchestrated as an experiment to observe how effectively these methods could function outside controlled laboratory conditions.

The speculation gained credibility in 1978 when the CIA's Deputy Director sent an official letter to Congressman Leo Ryan, explicitly acknowledging that mind control experiments had indeed been conducted on volunteer inmates at Vacaville, though the agency claimed the program had ended in 1968.

Yet questions persist about whether all CIA activities at the facility truly ceased at that time. The connection between Vacaville and mind control becomes even more intriguing when considering another infamous former resident: Charles Manson.

Manson, who orchestrated one of the most shocking murder sprees in American history, employed remarkably similar techniques to those developed by the CIA—specifically, the combination of LSD and hypnotic suggestion to control his followers. The fact that both he and DeFreeze spent significant time at Vacaville, and both later demonstrated sophisticated knowledge of psychological manipulation, strikes many observers as more than mere coincidence.

Adding to these suspicions, California established a Maximum Diagnostic Unit at CMF in 1972. This experimental psychological program worked with carefully selected inmates from among the 700 individuals held in solitary confinement throughout the state prison system. The timing—just four years after the CIA claimed to have ended its Vacaville operations—raises obvious questions about whether the intelligence agency had simply rebranded its research under state oversight.

Whether these theories hold any truth remains a matter of speculation. What cannot be disputed is that Vacaville served as a site of documented government experimentation on human subjects, and that several individuals who later demonstrated unusual expertise in psychological manipulation spent formative periods within its walls. The full story of what occurred behind those walls may never be known, but the questions it raises about the intersection of government power, scientific research, and human rights continue to resonate decades later.

6
TRANSMISSION

SUNLIGHT FILTERS through the blinds on Tuesday morning with a new brilliance. The world is in deeper focus, its edges sharpened down to the atoms. Though she still has to work out all the details, June now has a plan, and the plan gives her purpose.

Yes, when the time comes, she will have to do the deed, something she thought she would never be capable of. But she blocks those worries from her mind. For now, she wants to lose herself in the pull she feels in the pit of her stomach—like jumping off a tall building. She can learn to fly on the way down or crash into oblivion, but in the meantime, she's content with the wind in her hair. She hasn't felt this free in a long time. And that changes everything.

I can do this, she thinks. I'll kill the bastard.

It should be easy enough. All he ever does after dinner is watch TV and drink until he passes out in his stupid La-Z-Boy. Mom will have to work late at some point; she always does. Then June can just hold a pillow over his ugly face and finish the job.

Maybe she can do it before the Golden Week.

Getting away with it isn't the point, but who knows? Maybe

it will look like a heart attack. Natural causes. It's possible; he's not healthy to begin with. Then she will be free of him forever, no matter what her stupid mother says. Sorry Mom, you had your chance to fix this.

June has the radio on, tuned to Sacramento's new wave station, KWOD 106.5. The drums and guitars of "Head On" by The Jesus and Mary Chain fill her room. June feels as if she's been held underwater for an eternity and is only now coming up for air. This is the new June. She's not powerless. Keep On Keeping On isn't enough—sometimes you have to take control and make your own luck. She spins and dances around her room.

When she reaches out to turn up the volume, she sees sunlight glinting off something silver lying on her nightstand. It's her lucky bracelet, the one her father gave her when she turned fifteen. A silver replica of the plastic bracelet her parents made her wear all the time when she was little. Around the inside is the inscription that always makes her cry:

To June, you will always be my little girl. Love, Dad.

The original bracelet had her address imprinted on the inside in case she ever got lost, and a shortened version is here, too. It became a reminder of her father and the fact that she would always have a safe place to come home to, if need be. She puts the bracelet away in her jewelry box.

A quick sniff of her armpit doesn't reveal any smells. Good, no need to shower today. School is only a means to an end; she doesn't care what any of the kids in class think of her, though she does need to get dressed. She fumbles around in her underwear drawer and finds the tube sock with her money stash.

Something is wrong. Confused, she pulls it out.

Shit.

It's way too light. She pulls at the end and dumps the money on her bed. Hands feverishly divide the bills into piles of varying denominations. It doesn't take long to count it all. Her mouth hangs open in shock. Half of it is missing.

Half the money she's been saving since she was sixteen is gone. Evaporated. It doesn't make any sense. Who could have done this? No one else comes into her room, and they hardly ever have company over. Sure, Bree comes by often enough, but she is like a sister to June—she almost doesn't count. And June knows all of Bree's secrets. Being a kleptomaniac isn't one of them.

That only leaves three possible scenarios, all of them terrible. Either it was her mother, it was Randy, or it was both of them working together.

Her mother is an awful liar, so that would be easy enough to figure out. It's the best place to start.

June finishes getting dressed and goes downstairs to the kitchen. Mommy dearest is in the middle of her morning routine, making her lunch for the day. A ray of sunlight glints off the knife as she cuts her sandwich in half. She looks up as June walks in.

"You look different today, what is it? Your hair?" Gail looks June over with a mother's discerning eye. "Wait, did you meet a boy? This is about a boy, isn't it?"

"You could say that," June says as she grabs a box of cereal from the pantry.

"Hey, do you have a ride to school?"

"Yeah, Bree's coming by in about twenty minutes, but she's going shopping with her mom after school, so I don't know how I'm getting home yet."

Gail's face brightens. "Oh! I'll have Randy pick you up. He needs to get out of the house, anyway."

Oh god no. June stiffens. She opens her mouth to respond, but Gail crosses her arms.

"Remember, team player, right?"

June suddenly has the urge to slap her mother in the face. She looks away and makes it sink down to the dark place inside her, mumbling, "Okay, whatever." Her stomach feels sick. The thought of being alone in a car with Randy makes her want to stab herself.

"See?" Gail says in a condescending tone. She puts her sandwich in a bag, picks up her keys, and slings her purse over her shoulder. "Everything's always so dramatic with you teenagers. Things aren't really that bad, huh?"

June reaches out and touches Gail's arm. "Mom, I have to ask you something."

Gail glances at the microwave to check the time. "All right, I'll give you two minutes."

"Mom, it's important."

"What? I said two minutes."

June blurts out about the stash of money she keeps in her dresser. She knows it may come as a surprise that she was hiding money from her, but June needs to see how Gail reacts. It's the only way to know for sure if she was in on it.

Gail suddenly gasps for air. June doesn't know what to expect, but this is anything but subtle. There are no feeble denials, no cries of righteous indignation. Once she gets her wind, Gail's reaction is pure shock and rage.

"How long?" she says through clenched teeth, making June wince at the sudden viciousness directed at her. "How long have you had that?"

June looks down at the tile floor and says in a low voice, "Since Dad died."

"Before Randy, we were starving, and you were holding out on me? You had money hidden somewhere this whole time?"

June looks away; she doesn't see it coming.

SMACK.

June's right cheek feels like she's being stabbed by a thousand hot needles. She puts her hand to it and thinks: Maybe I'll kill you both.

Even though her mother is glaring fireballs at her, June wills herself not to react. She knows how these things escalate, so she just stares straight ahead at a small crack in the wall over her mother's shoulder.

Gail's narrowed eyes flick back to the clock. She sighs and turns to leave through the garage, muttering something rude under her breath.

June digs her fingernails into her hands as she waits for the car to start. The garage door rolls up with a small thunderclap; Gail backs out, then drives off down the street. June can barely breathe, and she's too sick to eat. She pours her cereal down the drain and deliberately runs the garbage disposal extra long, hoping to annoy Randy as he sleeps off another one of his benders.

She grabs her backpack and goes outside to sit at the curb. Bree will be here soon, but not soon enough. June digs her nails deeper into her palms again; it is all she can do to keep from crying. The slap was humiliating, but worse was how stupid it makes her feel. Who is she kidding? Her plan will never work.

Randy deserves to die, there is no doubt about that. But does she really have it in her to kill someone? To kill Randy? She has the desire, but it's all too much. Everything is crumbling apart around her. She doesn't know where her misery ends and the rest of the world begins anymore.

What if she gets caught—could she spend the rest of her life in prison? Would it be worth it? And even if she got paroled, would she ever be able to get a job, have a normal life as a convicted felon? But the alternative is no less terrifying: Will she ever have a normal life anyway if Randy gets his way? Her head is spinning and now both of her palms are bleeding.

As if things would ever be that easy. Like she could murder Randy and still have a summer with Bree. Still finish high school next year. Still keep her life in Cowtown intact. Her mother would probably just find another Randy. No, nothing here will ever change.

June tries to push these thoughts away, but it is getting harder and harder to keep her head straight, and she still has the rest of the day ahead of her.

School.

Shit, she still has to go to school and somehow fit in with everyone else. It's all so exhausting; she hates putting on a mask every day for school and work. Sometimes she feels like her whole life is a lie.

So Gail didn't take the money. She didn't even know about it. Which means only one thing: Randy took it. All by himself. It had to be him. Then June's pulse quickens as she realizes the horrible truth underneath. How did he even find it, anyway? How would he know where to look? June never told a soul about the money stash, so he couldn't have overheard anything. He must have stumbled upon it because—

Because he was pawing around in my underwear drawer? He was fondling my panties when I was off at school?

She dry heaves over the pavement.

As the world blurs out of focus, she can't stop thinking: I've got to do something. Can't stay here. Not now. Not anymore. Mom is useless. And Randy... oh God. Maybe I'll just have to run away.

7
THE MIGHTY QUINN

ALTHOUGH THE MAXIMUM Diagnostic Units were few, Vacaville was not the only location in the United States for such an experimental endeavor; however, there were never as many as the conspiracy theorists claimed. Some units are still in operation, hiding in plain sight, scattered across various facilities around the country: one in a major city hospital, one masquerading as a non-profit mental health group that consults for several federal prisons, and two psychiatric wards adjacent to military bases. But there is another that's always been kept a closely guarded secret.

Nearly twelve hundred miles from Vacaville—near Santa Fe, New Mexico—stands the facade of a special facility, a towering monolith of chrome and glass that dominates a government complex on the southeastern edge of town. The Bellhaven Chambers Institute, often simply called the Bell, is named for nineteenth-century experimental psychologist Charles Bell and primary benefactor Margaret Chambers, whose family trust provided the initial funding in the 1960s. The "haven" was added to reflect the institute's stated mission as a sanctuary for advanced psychological and medical research.

Sometimes, as the sun beats down on the merciless New Mexico desert summer afternoons, workers near the site will look up at the sun reflecting off the mirrored monstrosity and say, "Oh, God's ringing the Bell again." Of course, this is just tradition. Those who witness what goes on in this building (and in the tunnels below) are not long for religion.

Black marble floors and counters fill the Bell's interior while technicians in white lab coats scurry about the halls, creating a low hum of constant activity.

During the day, a woman sits behind the counter in the lobby —young, pretty, and vigilant in her duties as gatekeeper to all who enter the building. If you were to walk in, she would ask your name as she consults her computer. If you're fortunate, she would smile politely as she says that you do not have clearance. Guards would appear and escort you outside, and from there you would simply go on about your life.

The unlucky ones? She would give them a knowing nod and then call for a supervisor, who would come and take them inside the facility proper. No one, other than staff, is allowed in the building without a floor supervisor escorting their visit.

Then there are those with an elevated level of misfortune. A guard would take them over to one of the long line of elevators, down to the deepest levels of the secret underground lab. They would ride a cart about a mile east to the heart of the operation, where all the real work gets done. The Powers That Be learned their lesson at Vacaville. Some things are better left unknown. Thus, a new Maximum Diagnostic Unit works in utmost secrecy; its code name is MDU-00S-7. The only eyes that ever see this work are the lab technicians, the floor supervisors, the guards, and the test subjects themselves.

It is here, at a desk tucked into a dimly lit alcove at the south-ernmost end, where MDU-00S-7's newest security guard absent-mindedly taps his foot on a muggy summer morning in mid-June. On the corner of his desk sits a small, tin-looking radio that looks like it was made in the '60s. The Rolling Stones' "Jumping Jack Flash" plays barely above the din of the servers and air conditioning.

A middle-aged African-American man approaches and sets his coffee cup down on an adjacent desk. He turns to the new guard and says, "Tom Quinn?"

"Yes, sir."

The older man laughs. "No, there's no sir here." He holds out his hand. "Jack Dawkins. Welcome to the Bell. Officially, the Bellhaven Chambers Institute. But nobody calls it that."

Tom Quinn shakes his hand. "Thank you, si—." He smiles, catching himself.

His new partner gives him a look of recognition and respect. "I know where you're from, but you're not in the service anymore. This here's just a job. And if we do it right, nobody gets hurt. At least, that's what they tell me."

"How long have you been working here?"

"Long enough." Jack Dawkins points to the little radio. "How'd you get that to work? Can't be any reception down here."

Tom lights up; he loves talking about computers. "Oh, I've got it hooked up to my PC. It's acting as a sound monitor now." He beams and points to a bulky gray box next to his monitor. "It's called a CD-ROM drive. I'm playing a CD *through my computer*."

"Huh," Jack, who has no mind for machines, quickly loses interest. "What will they think up next? Well, that's probably why you're here. We need somebody to reboot the servers when they go down."

"Do they go down a lot?"

"More than a cheerleader on prom night."

Since it's his first day, Tom keeps the volume of his music low; he's not sure if this sort of thing is allowed here. He nods at his little radio. "Do you think that's okay?"

Jack chuckles again. "Man, ain't nobody gonna bother you down here. Only faces you'll ever see—besides the subs, that is —are my ugly mug and Anders, of course." Erik Anders is the floor supervisor for this level of MDU-00S-7.

Tom's cheeks flush red. He hates being the new guy, hates having to admit he doesn't know anything yet. But he has to ask. "You said subs. What are subs?"

"Man, didn't they tell you anything up there in orientation? The subjects, man. Or patients, if you want to call them that. You stay here long enough, you'll see some shit that's gonna blow your mind. Turn you upside down, like finding out there's no Santa Claus. You know, it's not too late, you can still jump ship. Take the elevator up, tell them it didn't work out, and walk right out the front door. Pretend you were never here. Shit, I would if I could." Jack sits down in his chair and starts logging into his computer, saying over his shoulder, "That's what I say."

"Can't. Need the money."

"Me, too. Ain't that a bitch."

"And the insurance," Tom adds.

"Double bitch."

Tom has a hard time sizing up his new partner, who could be in his early to mid-forties. He doesn't look like former military, though many of the guards upstairs are. Maybe a cop in a previous life? The hiring process for the Bell was brutal, with the most thorough background check Tom had ever seen. They don't take just anybody, not even for a security guard position.

Jack grabs the phone from his desk and dials a number. "Hey, get Brad." He waits a few moments, tapping his fingertips on the desktop. "Brad, yeah, gimme a marker for July 15th. The new guy down here, Tom Quinn. Yeah, the Indian." He hangs up.

Tom tries not to be offended. He doesn't want any trouble on his first day. Like he said, he needs the job. Maybe it's one of those things the old guards do—rib the new guy. Still, Tom has to at least address it. "Uh, Jack, what was that about?"

"Me and some of the guys upstairs got a pool going."

"For what?"

"For when you gonna bust your cherry. Everybody here tosses their cookies at some point. *Everybody*. Just a matter of time. Some even do it on their first day, usually right after lunch."

"Whatever," Tom waves it off, but then adds as an afterthought, "Actually, I'm Inuk."

"I thought you said your name was Tom."

"No, Inuk. The singular of Inuit. As in, native of Alaska."

Jack looks flummoxed. "Look, I didn't mean—"

Tom holds his palm out to stop him. "Really, it's no big deal." He sighs. "Indian, I get that a lot. People assume things, but you know how it goes. Hell, most people think I'm Mexican."

Jack laughs. "Right, and some folks around here think I'm just some negro from the streets." He straightens his tie in a purposeful gesture. "I went to Stanford, thank you very much."

Tom smiles. "Nice to meet you, Jack Dawkins from Stanford."

"Nice to meet you, too, Tom Quinn… Inuk or Into-It, or whatever you said. It's all good. We're all the same. We're all red and gooey on the inside, that's what I say."

Tom still doesn't know what to make of this strange man. He doesn't talk like he went to Stanford, but Tom is not in a position to judge—he knows he doesn't always act like a man who did two tours overseas. To each his own. He's just here to do a job and stay out of trouble. If Jack has running jokes with his friends upstairs, he can have them, along with his street talk and vague innuendos about this place.

Jack grabs a clipboard from his desk and flips pages over as he reads. "Our docket today says we gotta do inventory. For the whole south block. We better get going."

"Inventory, sure. So what are we counting?"

Jack looks down the hall with no expression on his face. "The subs, man. We're counting people."

8

HELL IS FOR CHILDREN

JUNE SLEEPWALKS through the day at school, shuffling her feet from class to class, mindlessly sitting through one useless lecture after another. None of this means anything to her now.

Third-period history is a blur. That prick, Mr. Sampson, seems to glare at her during roll, as if he suddenly forgets her name. Then he wheels out a metal stand with a TV and VCR to the front of the classroom, smiling the whole time, like he's doing the class the biggest favor in the world.

"We're having a movie today. *Gandhi*." He gestures to the back of the room, saying, "And yes, this will be on the test." Since there are only a handful of days left in school and they have already taken the final, everyone giggles. Everyone except June.

"Shouldn't have any objectionable content, not that I know of. If any of you have a problem with it, you can always go to Room 6 for study hall. Any takers?" His eyes sweep over the class and settle on June. Everyone gives her sideways glances.

She slumps down in her seat and looks straight ahead, focusing on the television screen behind Mr. Sampson reflecting his bald spot. He sighs and mumbles something under his breath, turns on the TV, and pushes the VHS tape into the player. June closes her eyes and prays for everyone to just leave her alone. They do.

Walking through the halls between classes feels like a delirious pilgrimage through a desert, her feet sinking deeper into the sand with each step. She doesn't remember getting to her locker; she just looks up at one point and there she is, with everybody staring at her like she has three heads.

"What's up with you?" Bree asks, brushing her hair in front of a little mirror in her locker. She looks back at June through the mirror. "You look like a zombie."

There it is again. The sudden urge to slap someone, anyone— this time, Bree, who doesn't deserve it. Would hurting Bree make anything better? Of course not. These intrusive thoughts scare June; she doesn't know herself anymore. Maybe talking to a therapist or psychiatrist would help. She considers looking into that. As soon as she sorts out the 1,004 other things that are wrong in her life.

As soon as she kills Randy. Or finds a way out.

"Nothing," June says. "I'm fine." She goes to close her locker but accidentally slams it shut with a bang. "Sorry," she says, biting her lip.

"No worries." Bree looks over June's shoulder. "Oh shit, it's C.S."

A skinny girl with jet-black hair down to her shoulders saunters up between them. She wears a short-sleeved white dress shirt with too many buttons undone over a tight black pencil skirt. She's not carrying any books, just a little black purse dangling over her shoulder.

"Hi, Cassandra," Bree says between clenched teeth.

June and Bree both bristle. Cassandra Stevens is the closest thing Vaca High has to a girl bully. Unless you're one of the most popular girls in school, you don't want to cross paths with her. A group of cheerleader sycophants who coo at her every word constantly follows her around, but surprisingly, she is sans entourage today.

"Wow, your hair looks so hot, June." Cassandra runs her fingers through the bottom strands of June's red hair.

"Yeah, that was almost sincere," Bree says. "So close."

"No, really. I mean it. That color looks great on you. For once." Cassandra saunters away, then calls back over her shoulder in a voice that oozes with bitchiness, "Your mom's going to have to get a really big broom to beat off all the boys this summer."

June narrows her eyes as Cassandra slinks away down the hall.

"Ugh, hate her," Bree says, slamming her locker shut too hard on purpose. "Not sorry."

June puts her hand over her mouth and giggles.

"What?" Bree asks.

"She said, '*Beat off.*'"

They both burst out laughing. For the first time since her mom's slap this morning, June thinks she might make it through the day.

Good old Bree, always a shoulder to lean on, but June's second wind is short-lived. When the bell rings at the end of sixth period, June has to fight back tears as anxiety washes over her. Here we go: time to be a team player.

Students file out of the building, the hum of their chatter and laughter filling the halls. June holds her breath as she walks past the office near the school's main entrance. Howard Zinn—a senior with short brown hair who always smiles at her whenever they pass each other in the halls—walks out. He looks back and holds the door open for her. She thanks him and smiles, making a mental note to ask if he'd want to join her and Bree for *Bill & Ted's Excellent Adventure* on Friday night.

BANG.

She smacks into a brown trash can right outside the door. Something green leaves a smudge on the front of her jeans. Howard turns back at the sound. June shrugs and gives him a look that says: *What can you do?* At least he's not laughing in her face.

But someone is laughing. June looks past Howard; Cassandra Stevens is leaning against the railing along the walkway, holding her stomach and pointing. Girls who all look like models start giggling and whispering to each other.

June looks away and forces a smirk across her face. She won't let them get to her, even though inside she doesn't think this day could get any worse. But then she turns to the parking lot and her face falls.

It's worse.

There it is—the douchemobile—and inside is Randy's fat face, beaming with a shit-eating grin, parked by the curb under a "No Parking" sign. He waves and pushes his Ray-Bans up the bridge of his nose with his middle finger. What an asshole. He sniffs the air like a starving coyote, ready to devour every girl within a five-mile radius.

June slips into the passenger seat without looking at him and mumbles, "Thanks." She has nothing else to say to him, except maybe: Die.

Randy starts the engine and looks over at her. "No problem, June-in-June. No problem at all."

She pulls her hair over the side of her face; she can't stand his gaze. But he is looking beyond her at the school entrance. Cassandra is still there, talking with her friends who act like they all belong on magazine covers. One girl is bending over to tie her shoe; her skirt is riding up, revealing a milky white thigh.

"Mmmmm." Randy lowers his sunglasses and squints his eyes. "I'm going to have to pick you up more often."

June's queasy stomach makes her glad she missed lunch.

He guns the engine, then pulls out. After shifting gears, his hand grazes June's leg. She closes her eyes and counts to ten— it's all she can do to not scream at the top of her lungs. Biting her lip, the coppery taste of blood penetrates her mouth as she reopens the wound from yesterday morning.

As much as she hates Randy, she can't start a fight. Not now. She doesn't need another talk about being a team player. Fuck this team. June knows by now that some things simply have to be endured, though she might explode any minute. She doesn't know how much more she can take.

As soon as they get home, June rushes to her room and shuts the door. She needs to be alone, has to calm the maelstrom of thoughts and emotions swirling inside her.

A couple hours later, a key scrapes into the lock on the front door; it creaks open. Her mother is home from work. She usually makes it home by evening, but her boss is notorious for messing with her schedule at a moment's notice.

June waits in her room until she is called down for dinner. She takes one look at the table and wrinkles her nose. Fish sticks and fries. Mom is always beat after work—who wouldn't be?— but this is so white trash. Of course, Randy can't be bothered to help with anything around the house, let alone make dinner. Even though he's been home almost all week, and maybe the rest of this month, too.

Gail opens the door to the garage and calls out, "Honey, dinner."

The big garage door rumbles down to a close. Randy stomps in, reeking of motor oil and barely contained rage.

"Aw, hell."

"What?" Gail says, already getting defensive.

"Did you know you have a flat tire?"

"I didn't see it," she says in a small voice. "I just got home and made dinner."

"It's always something in this house!" He yells. "Everything we buy turns to shit. I don't have time for this, goddamnit." He looks up and sees the dirty look on her face.

"These days," she says, "you've got nothing *but* time."

He holds up his palms in a placating gesture. "Okay. All right, I'll take care of it. Geez." He washes his oily hands in the kitchen sink, shouting over the running water, the anger draining from his voice. "But it'll have to wait till tomorrow, too late to deal with it now. And there's a Kings game on tonight. Come on, it's the playoffs."

"As long as I can make it to work in the morning. You'll have to drop me off. It's a big day tomorrow, we have to count all the inventory for the summer. Going to take forever. One of those don't-wait-up-for-me nights."

June grimaces at the thought of being home alone with Creepy Randy.

"Hey, what's up with June's car?" Gail asks.

"It's not ready yet. Needs a new carburetor. I'll have it up and running soon, real soon."

June sits down and holds her head in her hands.

Gail says, "Anyway, can you pick her up from school again? And June, be a doll and do something about dinner tomorrow. It'll just be you two."

"Don't worry," Randy says, taking his seat at the head of the table. "I'll take care of your little girl." He looks away, but June can see a glimmer in his eyes and a slight smile that makes her skin crawl. He is way too happy about this.

Then he does it, the thing that makes the whole world unravel. He turns to her and winks.

June swallows hard. That can't have just happened. She must be seeing things. Unfortunately, Gail was watching the news; she couldn't have seen it.

"I'll take good care of her," Randy says, then adds under his breath, "real good."

June's mind is in denial, but her body knows the truth; bile wells up in her throat and she breaks out in a cold sweat. She realizes with mounting horror that he won't be getting drunk and passing out on the couch this time. He has other plans.

June chokes.

"You okay, honey?" Gail asks, patting her on the back.

"No, I don't feel so good."

"Why don't you go upstairs and lie down?" Gail turns to Randy. "She's sick again, I bet. I hear there's something going around."

"There always is," Randy says, popping a fish stick in his mouth, crunching loudly.

June trudges upstairs to her room as the panic attack sets in. Her pulse races and white spots dance before her eyes. It feels like a heart attack, but she knows it's not. The fact that she knows the drill doesn't make her crushing anxiety go away any faster. She closes her eyes and tries to focus on just breathing. Eventually, the cold sweat dries on her skin and she begins to calm down.

She knows she isn't dying. Not yet. The thought of Randy's hands all over her isn't killing her; it's just making her want to die.

She has to do something. Can't wait until tomorrow. She has to get out of here before he forces himself on her.

She shakes her head bitterly. Who is she kidding? She couldn't kill anyone, not even a piece of shit like him.

Only one thing to do: get as far away as possible. She can't let him pick her up from school tomorrow. That would be too late. Because once they get home and they're alone…

Shit, this is really happening.

It's got to be tonight. But how? Her car is still in pieces in the garage.

She'll take her mom's car. Mom will understand. Someday.

No, June remembers. Randy said Mom's car has a flat tire. And of course, he's not fixing it yet.

Damn it. Think of something.

Fine. Make your own luck. Got to do what you can with what you have. There's only one other option—she'll take Randy's car. Fuck him. He deserves it. Maybe she'll drive it right into a wall.

9

DRIVEN TO TEARS

TOM QUINN GETS into the passenger seat of the cart and asks, "It's too far to walk?"

"It is for me," Jack says, as he gets in and starts the engine by pushing a button on the black dashboard.

It's a mile to the front of the South Block. Tom holds a clipboard in his lap, familiarizing himself with the various checklists attached, wondering if he will ever get used to this. The cart's whining engine echoes off the smooth granite walls and high arched ceiling of the tunnel.

They come upon a small parking area in front of a windowed room, which Tom figures must be the entrance to the South Block itself. Jack almost hits a wall and brakes too hard.

Tom drops the clipboard. He gets out gingerly, rubbing his right thigh. "Nice landing," he says, relishing the chance to needle his partner. It feels like such a long time since his tours of duty—civilian life is a confusing mess of a world where he never seems to fit in. He longs to be one of the guys again. Regardless of what Jack said about not seeing many other faces on this job, Tom still hopes for a team atmosphere of some kind, one way or another.

Jack stands looking at the long windowed room with a faraway look in his eyes.

"Hey," Tom says, "is everything all right?"

After a pause, Jack walks to the door. He calls over his shoulder, "Sorry, got something on my mind. Grab that clipboard."

Inside is a foyer with a long black granite counter that mirrors the Bell's main lobby, but smaller and completely empty. They walk to the far end, the silence broken by the scrape of their boots on the tiled floor.

They enter a smaller antechamber, devoid of both furniture and people. Tom hears a dull murmur, perhaps from the air conditioning, and there are voices, though muffled. Tom's blood runs cold as he realizes he is about to see the subs. Whatever experiments are going on here under the Bell, Tom is about to get a good long look. He takes a deep breath and tries to relax. He doesn't know why he is so worked up; everything here should be perfectly above board. Nothing to worry about—first-day jitters, that's all.

Jack shrugs and says, "Let's get this over with." He opens the door.

A blast of sound hits them. The throbbing of various machines mixes with voices, like a crowd of people all talking to themselves in the middle of a storm, and a high-pitched whisper fills the air. Tom wants to ask what it is but thinks better of it. Best to let Jack lead the way, at least this first time through.

The room is a narrow space with glass walls on both sides. Along the walls are rows of small cells, each just big enough for one occupant. Lighting illuminates the glass, giving each room a soft glow with shimmering reflections. The ceiling is high, and at the end of the corridor is a door leading to whatever lies beyond.

Each cell houses a different test subject. The first four are animals: two dogs (they look like German Shepherds), a black domestic house cat, and a chimpanzee. None of the animals make any noise. The dogs and the cat are curled up and sleeping in their respective cells, but the chimp is wide awake. He stands motionless with his arms at his sides, staring at them with mournful eyes.

Tom is unnerved but forces himself to move on. Like Jack said earlier, they have a job to do.

All the remaining test subjects are human, some barely out of college, others well into middle age. At first glance, they all look normal enough, although most seem to be talking to themselves. Tom suspects that if their rooms are miked they might be able to hear each other, but none of the murmurings sound like actual conversations—just layers of overlapping incoherent ramblings. It doesn't appear that any of the subjects can see him or Jack. Tom stares, slack-jawed, at the scene, trying to make sense of it.

"Hey!" Jack yells over the din of the machines and the babbling voices. "Let's get a move on."

Jack takes the clipboard and makes a few checkmarks on the top sheet. He turns to leave, but before he can take a step, the young male subject in the nearest room repeatedly slaps the glass wall, leaving sweaty handprints in streaks that obscure his face. His brown hair is tangled and wild, sticking out from the sides of his head as if it hasn't been washed in days. His forehead glistens with sweat, and his cheeks are drawn tight, his eyes wide and desperate. Although the room's insulation seems to muffle his cries, he is clearly unhappy.

Other subjects react, suddenly aware of the commotion. Many begin to yell and scream, adding to the chorus of discontent. Tom cannot make out the words, but he gets the feeling that the subjects are now aware of their presence and are shouting obscenities at them. God, this feels like a prison. Some kind of experimental detention center. An older, balding man in the last room on the right rears up and spits; his mucus slowly drips down the glass wall.

"Jesus," Tom says, mostly to himself.

"Hey, this is all part of the program, I'm sure," Jack says. "We don't know what the higher-ups are working on down here or what experiment the doctors got going on. But it doesn't matter, because again, it's all part of the program. Man, they signed up for this. And we're just here to do our job."

Tom nods in silence, his face devolving into an unfocused, dazed expression.

"Are we going to be okay here?" Jack asks, looking Tom straight in the eye.

Looking away, Tom nods.

"No," Jack says. "I need to hear you say it."

"We're okay," Tom says, nodding again, adding in a softer voice, "yeah, we're okay."

They enter a second antechamber, lit by bright bulbs hanging from the ceiling, casting stark shadows across the black and white checkerboard tile floor. The room's walls are smooth cement. An imposing black table stands against the left wall with a large cathode ray tube monitor on top and a keyboard in front of it. Beneath the table is a row of PC towers with cables spilling behind them. The air in this room is still, a soothing quiet with only the low hum of the PCs. The system appears to be running a series of diagnostic tests.

Tom walks over to the table and reaches for the keyboard.

"No," Jack says quickly, "don't touch that. We never touch that. Leave it to the techs."

A water cooler stands next to a row of filing cabinets along the far wall. A drawer in the top row is open. Jack walks over and closes it, leaving Tom to wonder if he's being conscientious or if there's something in there he doesn't want Tom to see.

Jack notices Tom watching him and says "Someone could walk into that." He moves into the next room. "Come on," he calls back.

After years in the Marines, Tom is used to following orders. *Do your job, no questions asked* has been his life for longer than he can remember. He knows full well that there is always a bigger picture at play, and the grunts are kept on a need-to-know basis. Sometimes, there are things you simply do not need to know.

He remembers what Jack said earlier: "I know where you come from, but you're not in the service anymore. This here's just a job. And if we do it right, nobody gets hurt."

They trained him to compartmentalize his approach to this kind of work; still, he can't help but wonder what horrors they might be inflicting on the inmates here—no, not inmates, he catches himself. They're patients. Patients who, for some reason, do not seem free to leave if they wanted to. But Tom has only been on the job since this morning; to be fair, he has no idea what these people signed up for.

You stay here long enough, you're gonna see some shit that will blow your mind.

You're just here to do a job, he tells himself. Just follow orders, stay employed, and keep your health insurance. Maybe we can all get out of this in one piece.

"At least there aren't any kids here," he says.

Jack laughs. "Yeah, I know, right? Can you imagine what would happen if one of the subs got pregnant? Holy shit! I wouldn't want to be a part of that. I'll spend enough time in purgatory as it is."

Tom shakes his head. "I can't hear you over how bad that sounds."

"You think I'm kidding?" Jack says. "You don't even know, man. You don't know. But you will, you stay here long enough. Hey, I need you to do something."

He leads Tom down a corridor, where another wall of windows looks into rows of dorm-like cells. Single occupants in each. Similar demographics to the first corridor, but this time all the subs are human and lying down.

"Nap time," Jack says.

Tom nods. He doesn't know how they can sleep—the steady

roar of the nearby machines is intrusive, and the hissing is louder in this area.

"What do you need me to do?" he asks.

"There, you see that line?" A tube dangles down from the ceiling, next to a panel protruding from the far wall. Jack nods his head in that direction. "You hear that sound? I know you do. That's the leak. We gotta fix that shit. Go over there, hit the red button on that panel. Wait thirty seconds, then reconnect the tube and push the red button again. That should reboot the cycle. Go, do it now."

Tom does as he is told. The system comes back online, and the hissing fades. It might have been his imagination, but the drone of the machines seems to subside as well.

Jack walks slowly down the corridor, looking into each room and making marks on his checklist.

"Looks like it worked," Tom says. "What was that?"

"Oxygen reclamation system. Cleans out the carbon dioxide from the air, among other things. Most of the air is recycled this far underground. Shit builds up in a sealed-off section like this." He wipes his brow. "Good thing we came down here today. You know what would have happened if we didn't get that fixed? Shudder to think." Jack's chest heaves, as if in silent laughter.

Tom's mind reels. I am working with a madman.

They enter a third antechamber. The floor is a sea of black tiles that stretches out to the other side. Numerous tables are positioned around the room, each heavily laden with medical equipment. Syringes and scalpels gleam in a sterile white light, while stainless steel items glisten and radiate an unsettling still-ness. A long rectangular box in the corner hums softly and emits a chill that can be felt from across the room. Tom assumes it's some kind of refrigeration unit—what for, he can only guess.

Something nags at the back of his mind. He realizes what it is: the last three rooms from the previous corridor were empty. What could that mean? Were those rooms recently occupied? If so, did those subs opt out and get to go home, or did they die here?

In the last long corridor, the sub in the first room on the left is sitting up in his bed. Apparently male, judging by his stocky build, but it's hard to tell since he has no hair and burn scars cover his face. Grimacing, he closes his eyes tightly. His ears are misshapen holes, the skin curled around them red and swollen. Tom is afraid to look into any of the other rooms; he has seen enough madness for one day.

A loud, high-pitched scream rings out, sounds like it's coming from the end of the block. Once it starts, it doesn't stop.

"This can't be real," Tom says. "None of this is real."

Jack gives him a grave look. "Even if it's all in your mind, it wouldn't matter. The mind makes it real. One thing I know for sure, our job is real, and we've got to finish up if we don't want to hear it from Anders. Come on."

"You go on ahead," Tom says, a layer of sweat covering his skin. "I'll catch up in a minute."

"Take all the time you need, rookie." Jack pats him on the shoulder, then makes his way down the corridor, marking off the last items on his checklist.

When he reaches the end of the block, he rests his clipboard on his right hip and hangs his head.

"Shit."

Jack grabs his walkie-talkie from his belt clip. "Yeah, hey, it's Dawkins. We're doing a sweep of the south block." He pauses as a distorted voice responds. "No," Jack says, "it's not all right. We got a bleeder here. It's happening again."

White noise fills the air, then the distorted voice on the other end says something Tom can't make out.

"Yeah," Jack continues. "D23, the last room in D-section, on the left."

The distorted voice says, "What's gone is gone…"

Jack chimes in, "But the work goes on."

Tom stares down the hall at Jack's profile, thinking: What did I get myself into? He shuffles his feet, willing himself to make it to his partner at the end of the corridor.

Jack puts his walkie-talkie back on his belt and says over his shoulder, "She hasn't been feeling too well lately. I was afraid this would happen."

Tom turns around and faces the source of the screams. A heavyset woman with stringy hair is sitting on the floor, rocking back and forth with her arms across her chest. Her mouth quivers as she wails. Suddenly, she looks up, causing Tom to jolt back. She is bleeding from her eyes and nose, and a dark, mucus-colored liquid is oozing from her right ear. She picks at it, letting the mucus drip onto her shoulder.

Tom puts his hands on his knees and doubles over, heaving and taking deep breaths.

Jack instinctively backs away, then says into his walkie-talkie, "And bring a mop and a bucket. Before lunch? I think we got a new record."

10

HISTORY WILL TEACH US NOTHING

MOST PEOPLE THINK that teachers have it made. Must be a piece of cake, right? You get the whole summer off every year, plus spring break and two weeks during Christmas. Not bad. Who wouldn't want that schedule? It can't be much work. I mean, come on, you just talk to kids all day. And they're easy to control because you're so much bigger than them; of course they're going to listen to every word you say. Plus, don't forget, being in a union means job security.

Easy money.

Funny thing is, none of that is real. Except for the time off (which is sorely needed), it's all complete fiction, and Robert Sampson knows it. He knows it all too well.

This fantasy never materialized for him, nor for any teacher he ever met or worked with. Other than student teaching and maybe his first year (which now seems like a lifetime ago), this job hasn't exactly been a joy.

The harsh reality, working against his initial idealism, has turned his life's dream into year after year of drudgery. Add tonight to the list, as another long day turns into an even longer night, with more final exams to grade than he can stand.

He pours himself another glass of Pinot Noir and sighs. The work never stops, the recognition and accolades are nonexistent, and the kids are a jaw-grinding nightmare. Sometimes he dreams about them: stress dreams that shake him awake in a cold sweat. Most days, he feels more like a zookeeper than an educator.

Still, he needs to put these thoughts out of his mind and get to work. Tonight is too important. Right now, it doesn't matter how he feels; what matters is what he has to do, which is get himself out of this hole he has dug for himself. He's in real trouble, the kind of trouble the teachers union can't protect him from. Tenure isn't the golden safety net most people think it is.

And this time it's all his own fault.

He's procrastinated so much this year, but why not? All the kids do it. They're always complaining about not having enough time to do their homework, always asking for extensions—no, more like demanding them—and don't get him started about when the parents get involved. Their special little angels could never do any wrong.

He had to get his hair cropped short to stop himself from pulling it out. He still rubs his head when he gets worked up, which is all the time these days.

In the end, it's just more of the same bullshit: no one wants to do the work and everyone has an excuse. One year, a kid even tried the old "a dog ate my homework" routine. Sampson's jaw hit the floor. He couldn't believe anyone would be stupid enough to try such a worthless, pathetic line. Just tell me you didn't do the work. Be honest for once in your life.

Sampson wonders why he even bothers anymore. Giving the kids a break every once in a while just creates more work for himself. After giving too much ground to these mouth-breathers over the years, he had decided to never make that mistake again.

Do the work, or you'll fail. It's that simple. And no one cares who your parents are.

What do they do with their time? He's around these kids every day—different kids every hour, but somehow they're all the same. Their apathy has been rubbing off on him for so long, and this year it finally bled into his core; it got into him like a virus, a zombie virus, rotting his brain from the inside out.

But that's his own excuse, and it's way past time for excuses and recriminations. It's time for him to man up and take his medicine.

There comes a point when you can't put things off any longer.

Tonight he's going to have to do it. He's going to have to grade the finals for third-period history.

It could be worse. At least he's not completely negligent; he's finished grading all his other classes. But he couldn't face third-period history. That class is always too much of a chore, and it kills him.

He sits on the floor of his living room with his back to his gray couch. The papers are on the floor in front of him. He knows it will be a struggle to read them all, to try to make sense of the chaos. His head hurts just thinking about it. At least the class is all juniors; since no one's graduation depends on these grades, it's not the end of the world if he hasn't turned them in yet. It's really just a minor detail at the end of an awful, terrible year—but it's a detail his boss cares about. Unfortunately, his boss cares a great deal.

Principal McCallister runs a tight ship, and he's made it clear that if Sampson doesn't turn in these grades first thing tomorrow morning, it will be the end of his job.

He already granted him a second emergency extension, and his tone made clear how displeased he was with Sampson's minimal effort lately. He's not wrong. Graduation for the class of 1989 is Saturday; it's ridiculous for a teacher not to have his shit together by now.

He pops the cork on his second bottle of Pinot. His head is

buzzing from the wine, but he's not worried about his ability to finish grading; he's more concerned about his students' ability to explain themselves and present a cogent argument in their essay questions. He has long since given up on expecting complete sentences and decent paragraphs. These students write like they talk, as if all they do is watch MTV every waking hour. Even if he were completely drunk, he would still have more sense in his head than these kids do on their best day.

Not that it matters or makes much of a difference. He hasn't exactly shown good judgment himself lately, and this week is a prime example. That stupid, irresponsible lecture about Genghis Khan and the Mongols yesterday. What was he thinking? Of course someone freaked out. He couldn't blame her.

June Addison.

Maybe she's predisposed to such a reaction. Maybe something traumatic has happened to her. My God, what if she was raped? It's possible. The look on her face as she ran out of the classroom still haunts him. He can't get it out of his mind.

He only wanted to grab their attention; he never wanted to traumatize anyone. Who knows what the rest of the class was thinking? He's read most of their files, but he doesn't know the complete life story of every kid in that class. And he knows damn well that not everything in their lives is in those files anyway.

They are just kids. Sampson knows he needs to be more sensitive.

At least he didn't go on with what he had planned for the rest of the week. Wow, that would have been a disaster. No wonder all the other teachers show movies and play games during the last week of school.

Disgusted with himself, he tries to drown his guilt with another swig of wine, but there is not enough alcohol in the house to make this okay, not tonight.

Better get back to grading. There's always more to do, and

the work is never done. Being a teacher is like what they say about being a writer—it's like having homework every night for the rest of your life. Except as a teacher, you really do have homework: grading to slog through; lesson plans to make; endless bureaucratic paperwork, down to accounting for every photocopy you make all year.

It doesn't stop. And there's never enough time to get ahead of it all.

He smiles stupidly and raises his glass to no one. At least there's time for wine. But his smile turns sideways as he looks down at all the papers scattered around him. He knows he brought this on himself.

Why does he always do this?

———

Sting released a new album a couple of years ago—his second solo album after leaving The Police. The singles "We'll Be Together" and "Be Still My Beating Heart" are still playing on the radio; the Sacramento new wave station has them in light rotation. The rest of the album is pretty good, too, and there's a particularly interesting song on side two of the LP called "History Will Teach Us Nothing." It came to Sampson as he watched the kids in class scribble their answers during the final exam. An idea struck him, and, as it turns out, his own personal history continues to teach him nothing as well.

Once again, he has made more work for himself.

The memory makes him wince. Another sip of wine, a little deeper this time.

On a whim, he went to the chalkboard and announced to the class that he was adding an extra credit question to the final. "As you may know, Sting has a new album, and on it is a song called 'History Will Teach Us Nothing.'" He grabbed a piece of chalk and wrote out the song title on the board. "The idea is interesting enough, although I bet you can guess what I think of it," he said in a smarmy voice. Of course, no one got the joke from the only adult in the room. The kids just looked at him, pencils in hand, blank stares on their washed-out faces.

"So, according to Sting, history has nothing to teach us. Nothing at all. Apparently, I have wasted my life. You are the generation that will inherit the world one day. How do you feel about this quote? Do you agree or disagree? How will it affect your future decision making? Or will it affect your future at all? Explain."

He told them that their answers could potentially add an extra ten points to their final score. He also said that the person with the highest score on the final would get a prize: a gift certificate for two pizzas from Little Caesars. It was a birthday present from his ex-wife's sister earlier in the year. She did it just to be a bitch; she knows he hates pizza. Now he can't wait to get rid of the thing.

The mention of pizza got a mild reaction from the kids. Pencils hit paper.

Though they might try a little harder, Sampson knew this wouldn't magically make them smarter. He wanted to see what they came up with, but he wasn't holding his breath.

Now he puts his own pen to paper and begins to make a dent in his stack of exams to grade.

He gets through several of the finals, and it goes about as expected. The kids all do poorly. They checked out mentally earlier in the semester, as they do every year. Even Sarah Parsley, the butt-kisser, only gets 73%. The highest grade so far is from that glasses-wearing weirdo Todd Stansfield, who tops out at 84%.

It looks like Todd is going to take the prize, as predicted; no surprises here.

Sampson looks at his remaining pile of papers. God, not even halfway.

Shit.

He trudges on, his night never-ending. "Once more unto the breach," he says to himself, holding out his nearly empty wineglass in a toast. He downs the last of it in one gulp, then grabs more papers, wipes his forehead, and winces.

More bullshit answers, most of them predictable versions of:

History won't teach me anything because it's just boring facts. The only thing that matters for my future is getting rich and famous.

Sprinkled in are the smart-asses with their uninspired variations of:

History will teach us nothing because I hate history. It's stupid. Who needs it? The future is now.

Both hackneyed themes continue looping ad nauseam. Sampson shakes his head. Maybe he should just move out into the hills and live off the grid.

Half asleep now, his eyes feel puffy and heavy, like manhole covers stuck to his face. Too much wine tonight, but he's almost done. Ugh, just have to get through the rest of this mess. A shock bolts through him as he looks at the empty space to his left. Is this it? Please God, let this be all of them. But he knows he's been sloppy tonight, so he reaches under the couch, just in case something slipped under it.

He feels paper. Disappointment drips down his chest. But only one. One more, and this awful night can be over. One more, and he's another step closer to finishing this miserable week and even worse year.

He pulls the paper out from under the couch and looks it over. At first glance, the handwriting is neat enough, the paragraphs and spacing appear almost polished. He raises his eyebrows and looks for the name at the top.

It's June's.

Well, this should be good.

Good for a laugh, maybe.

Too tired to have any faith in her, he shrugs. Let's get this over with.

After a short time, he squints his eyes. She gets all the first answers correct. Surprising, yes, but maybe she got lucky. Now he almost wants her to do badly, if only to prove himself right.

She gets almost all the answers in the second section correct as well. Now he's starting to think she cheated. Damn, now he's going to have to go through all the exams of the kids sitting around her to check their answers again. Despair hits him in the gut. He doesn't know what to do. Should he let her get away with it, or stay up even later tonight to justify her potential failing grade for cheating?

Indecision wins, and he knows he has to at least finish grading her entire final before making any drastic moves.

He gets to the short-answer essay questions. A few clunkers in the mix, but most of them are technically correct. Her essay answers show clear writing and a decent grasp of the material, though not necessarily deep insight. Who is this girl? The answers are all in her own words, unique; he can already tell that the other kids' answers weren't like this.

Maybe she didn't cheat? She ends up with an 89%. Easily the highest score in the class. He didn't think she had it in her.

Now for her extra credit answer. Might as well cross that bridge.

Well, shit, this could go either way now. Turns out she is the only kid who gave a decent answer.

I just don't understand why we have to spend so much time learning about ancient history. The world is completely different now compared to back then. How is studying something like the Roman Empire supposed to get us ready for living in today's digital age?

It's wild. My friend's dad just bought one of those new Apple computers for their home! Can you believe regular people can actually have their own computer now if they can afford it? Not those old terminal things, but a real stand-alone computer. That one little machine is probably more powerful than the huge, clunky ones they used for the moon landing way back when. Crazy, right? It makes you wonder, if technology is advancing this quickly, what kind of world will we be living in by the year 2000? What could some history lesson from the 1960s really teach us about that?

I mean, I get that human nature with power struggles, wars, and all that stuff hasn't really changed over the centuries. The whole "human condition" thing and all that. But landing on the actual moon seems like it was a total game-changer to me. Plus the world is so intense and complicated these days. How could learning about cavemen help us understand any of that?

I don't know, I just feel like I need to keep my eyes forward if I want to be ready for the future coming my way. The past is important and all, but technology is moving so fast. We could be living in a whole new world soon. Hard to see how thousands of years ago can totally prepare us for that.

She even provided her own summary at the bottom.

Oops, I got a little off track there. Let me try to summarize what I was trying to say. I don't mean that history has no value at all. It's obviously still important to some degree. But I also don't think we can depend on it too much for understanding what the future will be like, you know? The world keeps changing in unpredictable ways that people in past eras couldn't see.

Does that make sense? Basically, I think history does matter, but it also has its limitations. We need to take lessons from the past, but also realize the world evolves in ways previous generations couldn't predict. So we have to keep our minds open and think independently about preparing for what's ahead.

Sampson is flabbergasted.

It's like he doesn't know her at all. He realizes he had her all backwards. Sure, her sullen attitude is atrocious, but she obviously has a good head on her shoulders. While June may not be the most dedicated student, she at least put in the effort to understand the class concepts and study properly for the final. Perhaps she has been applying herself all along, only surreptitiously. He just didn't see it. How could he be so wrong about someone who was right in front of him?

If she's had that mindset all along, it's on him for not seeing it and not helping her. And he was so hard on her all year—he just wanted her gone, as far away from him as possible. He has to admit that he was punishing her for his own mess of a life, and for what the school administration did to him by dumping so many kids in his class. But none of that was her fault.

Out of nowhere, a wave of nausea hits him. He puts the paper down and leans back on the couch, closing his eyes. The room spins around him, and he feels like he's going to be sick. He can't escape the thought of June's anguished face and how he must have looked to her, a monster towering over her, the way she fled the classroom in tears after his lecture on the Mongols. He should let her win the contest for that reason alone; it wouldn't make up for it, but it's the least he could do. The fact that she deserves it only strengthens his resolve. He'll announce it first thing tomorrow, and maybe apologize for his behavior as well.

He had decided against more wine tonight, but now he wants to pour another glass and let his mind wander. He feels as if someone has pulled the rug out from under him; his whole world has been turned upside down. He reaches for the bottle, but sees that it's empty. Open another? No, even he has his limits. With a sigh, he turns away from the empty bottle and heads to bed, hoping sleep will come.

He'll finalize these grades in the morning and turn them in when he gets to work. Then he'll find June to give her the good news.

Hope she likes pizza.

11

JUST A JOB TO DO

THE SKY TURNS from vibrant orange to deepening indigo as the sun vanishes below the horizon, casting long shadows across the bustling streets of Santa Fe. Tom Quinn navigates his old Ford Fiesta through the dense evening traffic, the rhythmic drone of his tires blending with the low thrum of "Every Breath You Take" playing softly on the radio. Beads of sweat trickle down his temples. Glancing at the dashboard, his eyes narrow at the temperature gauge creeping dangerously close to the red zone.

He flicks the switch for the headlights, but only the left one works. With his new job, maybe he can finally afford some repairs.

After a few blocks, he slaps the steering wheel in frustration. "What a mess." His first day working at the infamous Bellhaven Chambers Institute didn't exactly go as planned. He had higher hopes for his new position.

He thinks back to this morning. His day began well enough. How had things gone so wrong so fast?

When he'd first walked through the front doors, the cute girl at the reception desk flashed him a warm smile and handed him his badge. A welcome change from the stony faces he'd grown accustomed to in the service. "Here you go, Tom," she said sweetly, her eyes meeting his for a brief moment before looking away. He held his breath for a second, feeling like he was sixteen again on his first date.

The elevator ride up to orientation had been long, filled with several stops as people dressed in tailored suits and polished dress shoes got on and off. They smiled politely at each other, their voices a pleasant murmur of greetings and small talk.

One man turned to Tom and said, "Good morning, how are you?" A simple question, but it stirred something within him— hope that maybe, just maybe, he could get used to a place like this.

The elevator doors slid open. Beyond the hallway lay a large room that resembled a college classroom. Tables and chairs filled the space, with a whiteboard positioned expectantly at the front. New hires bustled about, claiming seats and exchanging polite greetings. Tom studied their faces, most of them young, probably fresh out of big name schools.

A heaviness settled in his chest as he took in the easy rapport between them. For so long, the only camaraderie he knew was the unbreakable bond that came from standing shoulder-to-shoulder with his platoon, lives constantly on the line. Here, it was a more civilized companionship, but no less alienating to an outsider like himself. Did he even belong in this new life?

A towering man strode into the room, practically buzzing with energy. "Good morning, and welcome!" he bellowed, kicking off the orientation with a slideshow about the Bellhaven Chambers complex. Tom stifled a yawn as the images flickered across the screen, his mind wandering. Could he really make his way here?

Finally, the lights came up. Polite applause filled the air, and

Tom hesitantly joined in, clapping softly even though there wasn't much to celebrate. He didn't want to stand out, to be the odd one in this sea of fresh faces. The room emptied with the muffled sounds of shuffling feet as Tom and the other new hires began their separate journeys within the Bell.

The elevator ride down was uneventful, except for the unnerving way the atmosphere changed as people got off at different floors. Their smiles slowly faded, replaced by increasingly sullen expressions and slumped shoulders. By the time they reached the lower levels, only Tom and another man remained.

"Almost there," the man sighed after several moments, glancing down at his watch before stepping off on the next floor. "Good luck."

Now alone, Tom rode the elevator to its final stop. He stepped out into a concrete hallway that seemed to stretch forever.

At the next stoplight, Tom turns up the radio while waiting behind a pickup truck, trying to drown out his thoughts.

"Come on, come on," he says, drumming his fingers impatiently on the steering wheel. The Police are still playing, but the thumping bass from the truck behind him overpowers the song. He glances in the rearview mirror and sees the silhouette of the driver swaying to the beat.

"All right, enough of that." He cranks up the volume higher, thinking of Jack Dawkins and wondering why he can't figure him out. It doesn't help that Jack laughed off all the rumors about the Bell.

"Ah, don't worry about that stuff," Jack said with a chuckle. "Just a bunch of nonsense cooked up by people with too much time on their hands."

Tom wants to believe him, but he knows better. Things are rarely that simple.

"God, what have I gotten myself into?"

As the light finally changes from red to green, Whitney Houston comes on the radio. He leans forward and punches the preset buttons, searching for something else, and settles on the Sex Pistols. He leans back, letting the wall of sound surround him.

———

Lunchtime had been its own ordeal. He was still feeling a little shaky from throwing up earlier, and the last thing he wanted was to draw more attention to himself.

"Hey, Tom," Jack said, with a big smile on his face, carrying his lunch tray. "Looking better, buddy. Don't sweat it, we've all had rough first days."

"Thanks," Tom said, trying to sound appreciative, though his face flushed. Jack sat down, and they watched a table across the room where two lab technicians were laughing at something one of them had said.

"Can you believe those guys?" He only caught bits and pieces of their conversation, but they were clearly joking about some experiment gone wrong. It felt surreal to hear them laughing after what he had seen today. Had the horrors of this place not affected them?

Jack saw the look on Tom's face and knew what he was thinking. "Guess they're used to it by now."

Tom wondered if he'd ever be able to reach that level of detachment.

He didn't expect to see anyone else down on their level. Jack had said earlier, "Man, ain't nobody gonna bother you down here." If that was true, then who were those two jokers having such a good time? And why did Anders barely acknowledge Tom's existence when he finally decided to show up?

———

Maybe there's somewhere else in the company I can move to, he thinks, watching as a lively group of friends pours out onto the sidewalk from a nearby bar across the street, their carefree whoops piercing the night air.

But where? And would they even let me?

His thoughts drift back to another thing that Jack said about just taking the elevator up to freedom and walking away. But is it too late now after what he's seen? Would they think he knows too much already? He rubs his right eye. The truth is, he doesn't really know anything. Nothing he saw today makes any sense to him.

He unclenches his jaw and eases his grip on the steering wheel. Tomorrow I'll start looking for a way out. One day at a time, he reminds himself.

A horn blares impatiently from behind. In the rearview mirror an old Chevy is riding his bumper, the driver's arm jutting out the window aggressively. Traffic has started moving again without Tom realizing it. He gives an apologetic wave of his hand and hits the gas.

In time, his tired eyes focus on the familiar houses lining his street, their windows glowing with warm light.

Pulling into his driveway, he hears gravel crunch beneath his tires. He kills the engine and sits in the stillness, gathering his thoughts.

"Okay, you need this job, you need the insurance. It's not all bad. You've survived worse, you'll get through this, too."

He knows he's grasping at straws, trying to find reasons to keep going back to that place, but what other choice does he have? Steeling himself, he pushes open the car door. The humid evening air wraps around him like a blanket. He grimaces, noticing his left tires are parked off the driveway and onto his xeriscaped front yard.

Things will look different in the morning, he thinks. Just get some sleep, and we'll figure it out tomorrow.

As he walks to his front door, he looks up at the night sky, stars beginning to dot the darkness above. In their steady light, he tries to find a glimmer of peace.

12
SHE'S LEAVING HOME

ON TUESDAY NIGHT, June stays in her room with the lights off, waiting for both Gail and Randy to go to sleep. As usual, Randy drinks too much and passes out in his chair while her mother reads a book in her bedroom. After dozing off for a few hours, Gail wakes with a start and goes downstairs to shake Randy awake and bring him up to bed. June has to make sure the coast is clear. She waits for another hour, then tiptoes down the hall and listens at the door—her mother is breathing steadily, and Randy is snoring loud enough to wake the neighbors.

She creeps back to her room to make her final preparations, though she has already packed her bag with her toothbrush and as many clothes as it will hold. The only non-essential item she allows herself is her special bracelet; she needs a reminder of her father to give her the strength she needs to see this through.

She takes a breath and thinks: I guess it's time.

A sudden panic stops her halfway down the stairs. She'd forgotten the most important thing. Chastising herself internally, she carefully makes her way back to her room.

The money stash is still in the top drawer of her dresser—well, what's left of it. She doesn't know where she's going, but she's going to need that money if she's ever going to make a new start on her own.

What is she doing? This is crazy; a decision like this is forever. She'll never make it on her own. Maybe, somehow, she's just overreacting. Maybe there's still a way to work this out.

But the thought of Randy licking his lips over the girls at school snaps her back to reality. An icy chill runs through her.

And her mother defended him! Was there any chance that Gail could be right? Sure, Randy takes care of them. They're not homeless or hungry or cold in the winter. But does that redeem him? Is doing one nice thing in your life enough to save you from being an asshole? You shouldn't get a medal for doing the bare minimum. Absolution could never be that easy; regardless, he can't just take what he wants.

He's not entitled to everything. He's not entitled to me.

Although the thought of never seeing her only living parent again is painful, she knows that her mother has failed her. June doesn't owe Gail anything. Bree always said June was too nice for her own good, and that went double where her mother was concerned. June was always worried about what Gail thought of her, always trying to make Gail happy at her own expense. No more. She's decided to put herself first for once. Since no one else will, she has to look out for herself, and right now, that can only mean one thing: escape.

She holds up the tube sock with the remainder of her money stash and ruefully assesses its lack of heft. Half of it is gone. Should she have been more careful? Maybe it's her own fault. She could have hidden it better. But she rails against these doubts; she knows she did nothing wrong. She worked hard, stayed disciplined, dutifully saved the money for so long. And they just took it. She seethes, resentful of how they can reach in and take whatever they want from her.

No, she shouldn't have to hide things in her own room. What's hers should stay hers.

Still, she knows if she takes this last step, there is no turning back. She also knows the world outside is a hard and cold place that won't stop spinning to give her a chance to pull herself together. No one is going to give her a break. June grits her teeth, her will unshakeable—she doesn't need anyone to give her a chance. She's going to take it anyway. Make her own luck.

Too much bullshit has gone on for far too long.

It ends tonight.

She makes her way downstairs, careful to avoid the third stair from the bottom that always creaks. Randy's keys are where he always leaves them: on the rung under the kitchen cabinet. She lets herself out and closes the front door behind her as quietly as possible, leaving it unlocked, not wanting to risk even that little click.

Randy's car door feels like the entrance to a bank vault; it doesn't close without a heavy thud. A dog barks from inside the house across the street. Why can't Randy drive a normal car like everyone else in the world?

She releases the parking break and puts the car in neutral, lets it roll back down the driveway under its own weight, turning slightly to get as far down the street as possible.

A deep breath. "Well, this is it." She turns the key, and the engine starts with a thunderous roar. Damn, it's so loud. Got to get out of here fast. She slams her foot down on the gas pedal; the force jerks her head back hard against the headrest. The stop sign at the end of the street comes too fast. She can't stop in time. She runs right past it, thanking the world that no other cars are out this late.

She wants to believe that a light goes on in her mother's bedroom; the curtain pulls back and her mother's face looks sadly out at the street. But in the rearview mirror, all remains dark.

It takes her a few moments to find the switch for the head-lights. She flicks them on and drives off into the night.

After a while, it all starts to sink in—she just stole a car. She has no idea when her mother and Randy might call the police, but the thought of being on her own, finally free to sink or swim, makes her skin tingle with the possibilities.

The rest of her life is a blank page; she can make it anything she wants.

She punches the radio on and turns it up loud.

13

KEEP ON RUNNIN'

IT STARTS off as a mad rush, every nerve in June's body firing as she guns the accelerator. The endless ribbon of highway blurs past as her headlights carve through the darkness. She blasts the radio, singing along. A world of infinite possibilities lies ahead, as boundless as the open road itself. Though her money is limited, she pushes the thought aside; she can worry about that later. Right now, all she has to do is leap into the great unknown.

In time, however, the rush fades to a dull ache in her back, leaving her with the stark reality of an uncertain world. Liberation alone won't keep her warm at night or put food in her stomach. She has to face the facts: it's well past the witching hour, there's no one to help her, and she has nowhere to go.

The concept of stopping makes her chest tighten, imagining the police already combing the streets, searching for her. Didn't someone once say sharks have to keep moving, even through the night, or they would suffocate? June doesn't know if that's true, but the idea resonates. If she's going to survive, she has to be like a shark—stealthy, ruthless, and always on the move.

In Sacramento, she takes the ramp off Highway 80 and crosses over the freeway, heading back to Fairfield. Until a better plan reveals itself, she'll repeat this pattern, looping back and forth all night, or at least as long as there is gas in the car.

A girl without a home, without a bed. Not that sleep would come easily anyway, her mind a whirlwind of frantic thoughts and unanswered questions. She takes a deep breath, forcing herself to inhale, exhale. Keep breathing, keep moving. The only thing she is sure of is she is never going back.

As the night wears on, fatigue gets the better of her. Around three in the morning, she takes the UC Davis exit, parking on a back road near the college campus. Climbing into the backseat, she curls up and tries to find a comfortable position. But her sleep is fitful, plagued by nightmares of monsters and people screaming, like it was the end of the world.

14

NOTHING BAD EVER HAPPENS TO ME

GAIL ADDISON IS PUTTING on eyeliner in her bathroom when she gets the second biggest shock of her life. She sees it out of the corner of her eye—a gray hair. This day is already off to a bad start. All she wants to do is curl up on the couch with a hot cup of coffee; it's way too early for makeup and gray hair. But work beckons, and like always, she's in a hurry. There are still lunches to pack and a daughter who needs to be reminded she has to get ready for school.

She pauses, listening. The house is far too quiet. June must be sleeping in again. That girl is going to be the death of me.

"Ow," she says, plucking out the gray strand with a pair of tweezers.

Randy, still in bed, sits up. "Everything okay in there?"

"Yeah, I found a gray hair."

"Just one?"

She turns and glares at him. "You need to get dressed. I have to leave soon and you're my ride."

"Hold your horses, Gail. I just need to put some pants on. You're in the way anyhow." He turns away from her and picks at his ear, then says over his shoulder. "And I still don't know why you have to go in so early today."

Gail sighs. "I already told you. It's a split shift. They need me to open the store this morning, then come back in the afternoon to get ready for inventory, which goes on into the night. You never listen." She leans her head out of the bathroom and calls down the hall. "June! School."

No response. Fine, we can do this the hard way. She marches over to her daughter's room, muttering under her breath, "If you're not ready in ten minutes, I'm going to—"

Gail throws open the door and shouts, "Let's go!"

The room is empty. June must already be downstairs. At least she made the bed for once, though a little too well—it looks like it hasn't been slept in at all. Gail tightens her lips when she notices June has left the top drawer of the dresser open. Then a curious thought occurs to her: Doesn't June have money hidden in here somewhere? But there is no time, not this morning. She closes the drawer and puts on her earrings as she heads downstairs.

"June?"

The living room is deserted, and the lights are off in the kitchen. What is going on? Where could that girl be? Maybe she's pouting and avoiding everyone this morning. It wouldn't be the first time she's done that. Maybe she's outside waiting for Bree. I bet she's out there and already found something to complain about.

Gail opens the front door and walks out into the yard. The street is almost empty; only a gray minivan is parked across the street two houses down. The paperboy whizzes by on his mountain bike and tosses out the morning edition, landing it on the driveway near her tattered slippers.

Turning back to the house, it hits her—something is terribly wrong.

Why was the front door unlocked? She quickly runs through

a mental checklist: Her car is parked in the garage with a flat tire, and June's car is still up on blocks next to it. Randy is upstairs lounging in bed, as he is every morning when he's home.

And yet the driveway is empty.

She looks back to make sure she's not losing her mind. His car isn't there.

All the air rushes out of her lungs. Her legs go weak and she plops down on the front steps. For about two minutes, she resists the urge to rush around in protest, bang on doors, and shout at the neighbors, the paperboy, anyone who would listen. But deep down, she knows the truth.

June is gone.

Gail lost her husband four years ago; she can't bear the thought of losing her one and only child now.

It was a Saturday night in December, a time from another life. In the middle of the night, the phone rang; Gail woke up alone. A male voice on the other end, a stranger, far too formal for such an hour. "Ma'am," he began. And just like that, she knew. Her whole life changed with the snap of a finger.

June was so excited to take her new car out for a spin. She drove all over town, but ended up at a house party thrown by some older boys she shouldn't have even known. Though quite the teetotaler now, June drank in those days, and that night was no exception. At least she had the sense not to drive home; she called her father to come and pick her up. Henry—God rest his soul—always told her to call anytime of the night if she ever got into trouble, no questions asked. And he always meant what he said.

But they didn't make it home. A drunk driver with no headlights on hit them as they drove through an intersection. Glass from the shattered windshield cut June's face. Then the car caught fire. They always tell you that only happens in the movies, but somehow it happened that night. Gail tears up again, thinking about the horribleness of it. They were trapped before help came. Henry was gone before they even got to the hospital. Gail didn't want to hear the details; she couldn't imagine such a thing. She had almost lost June then. Now she might have lost her for good.

That girl. She's never been on her own. How will she survive out there? Will she be okay? Will I ever see her again?

Gail grinds her jaw as despair turns to a dull bitterness. It's her own fault, she thinks. That girl did this to herself. All of it. If June had driven herself home that night, none of this would have happened. Henry was a good man, the best. He didn't deserve that. Lured to his death by his irresponsible daughter. Forever the ungrateful child. Never thinking of anyone but herself.

The wrong person died that night.

Gail longs for a Valium, for the numbness to take her mind away. There might be some left in the medicine cabinet. She doesn't want anything bad to happen to June, not really. If only the girl would mind her mother—but kids these days think they have all the answers. Maybe it's for the best if she finally learns a lesson or two about how this world really works. Gail's biggest regret is not taking her hand to that girl a long time ago.

There's nothing she can do about that now; there's nothing she can do about anything. Gail knows that she is not in control of her own house, constantly walking on eggshells around Randy, who can blow up at any moment over the smallest things.

The neighbor's rather large tabby cat, Chutney, shows up and promptly rubs up against Gail's legs. When he looks like he is about to run into the house, Gail gets up and goes inside, slamming the door in the cat's face. He simply moves on to rubbing against a fence post down the way, purring incessantly to no one.

. . .

Dazed, Gail drags herself upstairs to find Randy asleep again. Dust dances in stripes as the sunrise burns through the blinds. She wants to call out to him, but all she can manage is to mumble his name in a weak voice.

"Aw, geez, what is it now?" he says, rubbing his face. "Is that girl up yet?"

"She's not here."

He looks at Gail with bloodshot eyes. "So Bree picked her up?"

"No. She's not here."

"What do you mean?"

"She's gone."

"It's probably some school bullshit." He waves his hand at her in a dismissive gesture. "I'm going back to sleep."

"Not like this," Gail says, raising her voice now. She can't pretend any longer. It looks like June has finally had enough. "Something happened. I'm worried."

Randy starts a fake snore to tease her.

"How can you joke at a time like this?" Gail yells, then after a pause adds, "She took your car."

He bolts upright in bed, eyes wide open, a sneer forming on his lips. He chews his words. "What did you just say?"

"Your car. It's gone, too. Randy… oh God… my little girl is missing." Through all the resentment and blame, June is still her baby. Gail sits down on the bed and pushes her hair back, starts crying.

"Babe," Randy says, his voice softening, "let's give her some time. Maybe she just needs to cool off. Kids do this shit all the time. I'm sure she'll be back soon and we can work this all out."

"You really think so?" Gail bites her nails.

"Yeah, you'll see." He stands up and pulls on his pants.

"Where are you going?"

"I have to do something. Now you lie down for a spell and

I'll be right back. We'll call your boss, he can get someone else to open the store today. I'm sure he'll understand."

Randy pads downstairs, listening to make sure she's not following him. He goes into the kitchen and grabs the phone receiver from its wall mount. Dials a number.

"Hey, get the fuck up. Yeah, I'm whispering, never mind why. I've got a job for you. And no, you don't have a choice." He puts his hand over the receiver and listens again to make sure the hallway is quiet, that Gail hasn't somehow wandered downstairs. "Somebody stole my car last night and I need to get it back. Right fucking now."

The other man replies, but Randy cuts him off.

"No, the cops might be looking for it soon, and they can't get to it first. If you fuck this up, I'll…" He stops, hearing a creak upstairs. "Look, just fucking do it." He pauses while the other man answers again. "No, I know who stole it. Girl, nineteen, red hair, skinny little thing. She won't be much trouble."

The other man says, "When I find the car, what should I do with the girl?"

Randy sneers. "Kill her."

15

A DAY WITHOUT ME

"June, what are you doing?" It's Mr. Sampson, looking down at her like she has boogers all over her face.

Her head is down on her desk. Sore all over, she lifts her neck and looks up apologetically for having fallen asleep in class. The kids sitting around her in third period are giggling uncontrollably. One boy frames his face with his hands like he's holding a camera, making shutter noises with his mouth.

She looks down and freaks out. Oh my god! How did this happen? Bra and panties and burn scars all over. She must have forgotten her clothes at home—or gym class, but she's not even sure if she has gym this year. No wonder it's so cold. She realizes in a panic that she can't remember the combination to any locker she's had for at least the last three years. The kids are all laughing at her; the noise pounds through her spinning head.

She breathes in to scream—

June's eyes snap open; her piercing cry shatters the morning stillness. A flurry of wings and caws erupts from a nearby tree as startled birds take flight.

Her heartbeat pounds in her temples. Gasping for air, June blinks against the dim morning light filtering through fogged windows. Confusion takes hold as she looks around the unfamiliar interior of the car.

What happened? Where is she?

The heavy stench of stale air and gasoline makes her stomach turn. Her trembling fingers clutch the jacket twisted around her clammy body. A faint metallic taste lingers on her tongue.

Hazy memories surface bit by bit. Pulling over in the dead of night, crawling into the backseat… but the rest remains a blur. How did she end up here, alone in this car on the street?

The abrupt slam of a truck door outside makes her flinch. June's head whips around, strands of limp hair sticking to her face. Two lanky teenage boys amble past on the cracked sidewalk, backpacks slung over their slouching shoulders. Their voices carry through the closed window as they talk and laugh.

"Told you, dude, Evil Dead 2 kicks ass. Should've been there. What were you doing last night?"

"Your mom."

"Shut up, man. Whoa, something stinks. Did you shit your pants?"

"No, asshole. Must be a skunk or something. I hate having to park out here."

June sits unmoving in the backseat, staring blankly out the window as the two boys disappear from view. The world is still the same for you boys, she thinks bitterly, but you'll see. Life is just a series of random, cruel events. Nothing you can do about it. You never know where you'll end up.

A creeping sense of dread crawls through her as jagged pieces of flashbacks slowly knit themselves together. She already knows, deep down, that life as she knew it is over. But why? Then it all comes flooding back in stark, terrifying clarity.

Her breath catches in her throat as she realizes that she stole this car last night. Tears prick at the corners of her eyes. Oh God, what am I going to do? I don't even know where to go.

Again, the thought of going back home. Mom would know what to do. But the memory of Gail's stammering defenses of that bastard douses the impulse as quickly as it appears. No, never going back. Always moving forward. It's the only way now.

She wrinkles her nose as a foul odor refuses to be ignored. It smells like garbage. She looks around the car's interior, trying to figure out where it's coming from.

Another group walks by outside, three girls this time. They look directly at the car, whispering amongst themselves with furrowed brows.

Time to move on before drawing any more unwanted attention. June slides into the driver's seat and fumbles for the keys. Within minutes, she is headed north on the freeway towards Sacramento, leaving the residential streets behind.

Though it's still early morning, the summer heat is already building. The freeway stretches out before her in a seemingly endless, flat expanse baked by the relentless sun. And still, the rancid smell only worsens, becoming more pungent and overpowering by the mile. Even with her window rolled down, June can't seem to escape it.

Gritting her teeth, she tries to focus on the road, but a quick glance at the gas gauge reveals it's nearly empty. The old June would have panicked and pulled over immediately. But the new June feels a defiance coursing through her veins, a reckless determination to gamble it all, even when the odds are stacked against her.

So she presses her foot down on the accelerator, refusing to pull over until she either makes it to Sacramento or runs out of gas completely. It's a risk, but one she is willing to take.

In the end, June barely manages to coast into the city limits.

Luckily, it doesn't take long to find a gas station—they seem to be on nearly every street corner. The one she chooses has a small convenience store attached and a payphone mounted on the wall near the entrance.

When she sees the phone, a voice speaks in her mind: *Mom*. Yes, things would be so much easier if she had her mother on her side. But no, that's not her life anymore.

A stout, middle-aged man with a thick mustache stands behind the counter inside the store. June pulls out a crumpled twenty and asks for ten dollars on pump number six.

"No, that can't be it!" the man shouts in frustration, gesturing angrily at a small TV behind him, seemingly oblivious to June's presence. A woman wearing oversized glasses is struggling to solve a puzzle on *Wheel of Fortune*. "How can you not see that?!"

He notices June and her bewildered look. "Sorry about that," he says, handing her the change. "The people on these shows drive me crazy sometimes."

June offers a tight smile and starts to turn away, then hesitates. Pivoting back, she places a dollar bill on the counter. "Can I get some quarters, too?"

The thought of her mother sitting there with no idea what has become of her only daughter… it twists her guts into knots. The least she can do is call Mom and tell her that she is alive, that she isn't coming home. Despite everything, her mother deserves that much.

June pockets the quarters and heads back outside. She gingerly lifts the payphone receiver to her ear. Cold plastic, gritty with caked-on grime. She tries to wipe it clean on her sleeve, telling herself this call won't take long.

Closing her eyes, she draws in a steadying breath. When she opens them again, a college boy in a faded rugby shirt and tight jeans passes by, flashing her a warm smile and flirtatious nod. He has an athlete's body and easy confidence.

June's breath hitches as she instinctively returns the smile.

For a fleeting moment, she imagines a different world where meeting boys like this on a bright summer day is an exciting possibility, rather than a naive fantasy that is painfully out of reach.

The rush passes as quickly as it comes, her heart sinking back to reality. Those days are over now.

Ruefully, she turns back to the payphone, inserts a quarter into the sticky slot, and dials her mother's number. No use dwelling on what could have been. Regrets are a luxury she can no longer afford.

The washing machine churns to life, its steady rhythm the only reliable thing left in Gail's world. June is gone. There's nothing she can do about it, but the shock won't go away. She'd felt the initial anger burn through her, blur into confusion, and now crushing sorrow envelops her, threatening to swallow her whole.

She decides that if she can't stop the rush of anxious thoughts in her head, at least she can keep her body moving and get some chores done. The next load of towels sits in a heap beside her.

"Jesus Christ, do you have to do that now?" Randy shouts from the kitchen. He is rummaging around in the utility drawer, looking for tools. The coffee machine picked this morning to stop working—he's actually trying to fix something besides the cars in the garage for once.

Gail doesn't respond. She leans her back against the wall, slides to the floor, and begins to cry quietly. She can't deny it; she's not in control of what goes on in this house, and to tell the truth, she never has been. Despite what her daughter thinks of her, Gail has not had an easy life. She's been to the dark places in her mind often enough. But this time is different, infinitely worse. It feels like she is losing her mind.

Maybe now she deserves it. She has finally driven away her

only daughter, her baby, who couldn't take care of herself if her life depended on it. And now, apparently, it does.

Randy made her call in sick to work. She was honest and told her manager that her daughter went missing last night. He was less than sympathetic, didn't respond with any emotion at all, but he reluctantly cited something called FMLA and mentioned offhand that the company couldn't afford to get sued again. So he gave her one day off to get it together. When Gail hung up the receiver and immediately picked it back up, Randy stopped her.

"What are you doing?" he asked.

"Calling the police."

"Don't do that," he snapped. She gave him a look that could cut through steel. Randy put his hands up in a placating gesture. "Now... just—" He lowered his voice. "Sorry for getting short with you. I'm only saying we should think about this for a minute."

Gail hung up the phone and bit her lip.

"Don't they have to wait twenty-four hours to get involved?"

"I guess so."

"I'm sure she'll turn up," he said, then under his breath, "one way or another." He put his arms around her and spoke up again. "These kids today, they're always trying to blow off some steam. Maybe she just needs a little time."

Gail reluctantly agreed. When Randy focused on repairing the coffeemaker, she channeled her restless energy into cleaning the house and doing loads of laundry until her arms ached.

But now, sitting here, the questions won't stop: What can she do? Does anything even matter anymore? Going through the motions seems like such a waste of time, and not just the laundry. She's beginning to feel that way about her whole life. She wipes the hair out of her face and sighs. The washing machine pauses between cycles, and the ensuing quiet makes Gail hold her breath.

In the silence, there is hope.

And then it happens. The phone rings. It's like a stack of cymbals falling to the floor.

Gail leaps to her feet and runs to the kitchen. Randy holds a screwdriver in mid-air and stares at her; he has never seen her move so fast.

"Hello!" Gail yells into the receiver, then gathers herself and tries again at a normal volume. "Hello?" Inside her mind, she's screaming: *Please be her, oh God, please be her!*

"Hello, ma'am," says an older man's voice, deep and officious. Gail's stomach drops and her eyes well up with tears. He sounds like a policeman. Not again. *What happened to my baby girl?*

"No!" she screams.

"Well, ma'am, most folks at least hear what I've got to say before they answer, although I hear that a lot. May I trouble you for a few moments of your time?"

Gail doesn't react, just breathes into the phone and stares off into space.

"I'm a representative of the NorCal chapter of Blue Sky, a nonprofit organization that helps the families of local law enforcement officers who were injured in the line of duty. All donations are tax deductible per article 501(c)(3) of the Internal Revenue Code. Would you please consider—"

Gail quietly puts the phone back on its cradle and looks awkwardly at Randy. He shrugs and turns back to screwing in a plate at the bottom of the coffeemaker.

She sits down and puts her hands to her head, tries to make sense of her new broken world. Her home life has been balancing on a knife's edge for a long time. Deep down, she knew something would happen eventually, but she never thought it would be June who slipped first. As you get older, things crack and break apart; your life becomes a patched-up world. All you can do is duct tape it together as best you can. But some things you can't fix. Some things shatter and are gone forever. Tears roll down her cheeks, and she lets out a low sob.

She can tell Randy is watching her. He had stopped whatever he was doing and is now giving her the eye. Oh my God, what is he going to say now? Why couldn't he have been the one to leave?

"Gail, I know this is hard," he says in a soft voice, trying to be reassuring.

She's never heard him use that voice before; he sounds like a different person. Though caught off guard, she can't help but think: *No shit.*

"Think of it like this: it's like a game. Like a football game."

She stares at him in disbelief.

"Now, hear me out," he goes on. "Sometimes it comes down to the last second. And when the team goes for a field goal and the kicker misses, people always blame the kicker. Like he lost the game for them. But they've got it all wrong. It's not about that last second. The final score is about the entire game, including everything that came before. The whole team lost the game because it's about all of it, everything that happened from the beginning."

She gives him a weary look. "What are you talking about?"

He puts his hand on her shoulder. "It's not about this morning, or last night, or yesterday, or last week. It's about all of it. All the time you spent with her. And at a time like this, you have to trust yourself. It will work out. She's a part of you, and you're a part of her. If you really believe you've done right by her all along, she'll come back."

"You really think so?"

"She will. You'll see."

Gail doesn't know what's more surprising: that she's falling apart or that Randy is actually making her feel better. She's gotten used to his terrible attitude and mind games, but now he's suddenly being so nice. Could it be that he is genuinely coming around?

"You're a great mom," he says. "And you have strength. Now all you need is hope."

Gail clenches her jaw and lets the tears flow. He's really here for me, she thinks. He really does care. Maybe she's been wrong about everything.

The phone rings again, its shrill tone blasting through the room like a fire alarm. Randy tries to answer it, but Gail grabs it before he has a chance.

She listens for a second, then her expression changes completely. Randy doesn't have to ask who it is.

"Where are you?" Gail bursts out, her voice hoarse from crying.

Randy paces around the kitchen. He doesn't like not being able to hear this conversation. He doesn't like it one bit. Where is that girl? And how soon can she be back with his car? He needs to know what the hell is going on.

Gail sobs and mumbles something into the phone. Randy can't make any sense of it. Two stupid women and their emotional bullshit. Take care of this, Gail—or I'll take care of it for you.

"I just want to know you're okay," she says, lowering her tone, finally getting a grip on herself. "Honey, if you need some time, I understand."

No, no, no, this won't work at all, Randy thinks. I need that bitch home right now.

"Just come home when you're ready."

Randy walks over, presses his body right next to Gail, and gives her a hard look.

Confused, she puts her hand over the receiver and says to him, "What?"

Randy whispers, "Let's get her home."

"But you said…?"

His determined look doesn't change.

Her heart sinks. Heat floods her cheeks as her lips press into a thin, hard line. What happened to 'maybe June's only blowing off some steam?' He's the one who made it seem like this was no big deal. Why the sudden urgency?

She says, "I think we should let her be."

Randy rests his face close to hers, his voice low and controlled. "No, get her back. You get her home."

When Gail doesn't respond, he knows she's retreating behind that blank stare he's seen countless times before. He can't let her shut down now, not with June on the phone. "She has to get back. I need her here." He grabs Gail's chin, forcing her to look at him. "Get. Her. Back."

The words echo in Gail's mind: *I need her here.* What the hell is that supposed to mean? Why would he say that? What could Randy possibly need from her, besides his precious car? A cold fear shoots through her body. Something is very wrong, but this isn't the time to cross him. She reluctantly gives in.

"June, honey," Gail says, "on second thought, you should come home. It's time. You need to come home, sugar bear." She pauses while June responds. "No, no. Come home. It's for the best, you'll see. Come on, we need our little sugar bear home."

Randy stares at Gail, his jaw tight. Her shoulders slump forward as she listens to June. He does not like where this is going at all. Time to take control.

"Give me the phone," he says.

Gail flinches.

He raises his voice. "Give me the fucking phone. Now!"

"Randy, please," Gail says, her face in agony. "I just want to talk to my daughter."

"Give me the—"

Randy finishes his statement with the back of his hand. The receiver clatters to the floor. He scrambles to pick it up and straightens himself tall, puts it to his ear.

The line is dead.

16

TIME STAND STILL

JUNE STANDS OUTSIDE THE STOP & Go, pressed against the building to avoid the sun. She tugs at her sweatshirt collar, but the morning heat is already rising. Changing clothes is the least of her problems. Right now, she feels like she's been pushed over a cliff.

It meant a lot to her to call home, to make a genuine effort at some kind of amends, but the conversation fell apart faster than she expected. Gail's voice had an unsettling hollowness, making her sound like a stranger. She had always been guarded, but this was unnerving. And what was all that about "sugar bear?" It didn't make any sense. Her mother had never called her that before. Maybe it's some kind of sign, but of what?

When Randy cursed and started to lash out (like he always does), June knew she had to pull the plug. She said, "Sorry, Mom, it has to be this way," and hung up.

Now she turns around and stares off into the distance, raising her hand to shield her eyes from the glaring sunlight. Randy sounded wild, insane. Would he hurt Gail? Has he already? This whole situation is way out of control. This isn't the way things were supposed to be.

She picks up the receiver again and looks at it. Her hand fumbles in her pocket, compulsively counting the quarters she has left, but there is no one else to call.

Home was hell; she always felt trapped there, even before this current disaster. And here she is, ostensibly free—but with nowhere to go, she feels more pinned down than ever. Frustrated, she slams the receiver onto its wall-mounted base, then picks it up and slams it down again and again, shattering its plastic casing.

Her eyes well up with tears, but she holds them back, determined to keep it together. She can still hear Randy's voice in the background, his uncontrolled rage making her sick. She knows the truth. It was in her head all during the call, though she wouldn't let herself feel it. But now it sinks in.

She can never go home again. Not even if she wanted to.

June doesn't know what to do. Her eyes dart across her surroundings, desperate for an anchor point, something to ground her. The landscape offers only urban decay: candy wrappers skittering across the pavement in the wind, a dented soda can catching the sunlight, shards of broken plastic from the payphone. Then her gaze catches on a used condom against the wall near her foot. The gag reflex hits hard, but she is too dehydrated to do anything but dry heave.

Nausea rising in her throat, June stumbles back to the car. She tells herself she isn't going to cry anymore—not in this lifetime. She grips the steering wheel tightly, letting her sweat mingle with the leather. It's time to take charge, but truth be told, she has no idea how to do that. So she sits motionless, paralyzed by indecision.

Outside, life goes on, oblivious to her silent breakdown.

Then she notices it again. That smell. It's sharp and sour, with an underlying meatiness that turns her stomach. Something is definitely off in the car. It came to her in waves during the night.

She hoped it was just roadkill she'd passed on the highway, but the stench won't go away, and it's only getting stronger.

She looks around the front seats and back to see if maybe Randy left some food or something gross in here. God knows what has gone down in this car. But the inside is spotless except for dust on the dashboard and some dirt and blades of grass on the floor mats. This car is Randy's baby; he keeps it cleaner than the house.

She realizes with a start that she forgot what she came here to do. Needing to clear her mind—and her nose—she gets out and starts filling the tank with the gas she already paid for. The awning over the pumps provides a meager amount of shade, but she can still feel the California summer heat building relentlessly. A light breeze ruffles the leaves on a row of trees across the street. The fresh air helps her aching head, but after a few moments she scrunches her nose in disappointment—under the smell of gasoline, it's still there. The reek just won't leave her alone. She wants to think it's not a big deal, but it's there every time she breathes. It's as if something crawled out of the sewer and died in the car.

The numbers on the pump slowly tick up to her allotted ten dollars. When the handle clicks off, she puts it back and reflexively looks over the car.

The trunk. Never looked in the trunk. Maybe there's something in there?

With no cars behind her waiting for the pump, she has some time. She hovers for a moment with the key in her hand, anxiety running through her. Who knows what Randy is up to? Maybe some doors should never be opened. But no, she has to take care of this. If she's going to get anywhere in this car today, she has to know.

June pops the trunk and immediately puts her hand over her mouth to stifle a scream. She quickly glances around. No one near, no one to see this horror. She slams the trunk shut and hastily climbs back into the car.

"Ohshitohshitohshitohshit."

Despite the hot weather, a layer of cold sweat covers her skin. This can't be happening. She tries to convince herself it's a mistake, her mind playing tricks on her. But no—the smell is real, and the image is all too clear. Those few seconds stretch into an eternity, seared into her memory.

A body. Mangled and broken.

A man, probably middle-aged. His limbs were twisted and curled back. His skin was pale and bloated, like he drowned, though his clothes were dry. He was wearing a dark suit, his tie was loose, with the top buttons of his dress shirt undone. His face was contorted into a horrible, screaming death mask.

Behind the body was a duffle bag, military green, stuffed with who knows what. Underneath it was a mushy pool of drying blood. Dark marks around his neck raised terrible questions. Was he strangled? Hanged somewhere? How long had he been dead? How long had he been in the trunk?

And Randy parked this car in front of our house!?

What the hell is Randy involved in?

Panic takes over. June puts her forehead on the wheel and closes her eyes. She fears the worst—what if the police are looking for a stolen car and find that body in the trunk? Would they think she had something to do with it?

She looks up and knows she is sinking; her vision doubles, and all the surrounding sounds are suddenly out of phase: cars whizzing by, birds chirping in the trees down the road, a dog barking near the apartments across the street. It all sounds distant and distorted, as if she's hearing the world from underwater. It feels like the one time she tried smoking pot with Bree, wildly disorienting, except now it's all wrong and terrifying. She tries to focus on just breathing.

A quick glance inside the Stop & Go reveals the college boy, the one with the toothy smile, talking to the man with the mustache behind the counter. No one is smiling now. The stout clerk leans forward, as if to hear something better. What could they be talking about? Then the college boy points outside and they both turn their heads toward her in unison, synchronized like a bad MTV music video. Adrenaline surges through her, leaving her fingers tingling and her mouth dry.

The clerk grabs a phone and starts dialing.

June hears a voice in her head: *Better get out of here.*

She freezes, her fingers on the keys in the ignition.

The voice again, more insistent: *Get out of here, NOW.*

She starts the car and pulls out, almost hitting a white van coming down the street.

"I knew it!" she says, hitting the dashboard with her right fist. "I knew Randy was up to something." He could never have made all of his money in sales. It's absurd. Randy is terrible with people.

Did Randy kill that man? What in the world could he be mixed up in? Drugs? The mob? There isn't any mob in Northern California, as far as she knows, though there is gang activity.

Jesus, does Mom know? Has she been protecting him all along? Mom always seemed like an enabler, but this...

This is madness.

Definitely can't go home now. June needs to get out of town fast, as far away from this car as possible. Even if Gail reports her missing and the cops track her down later, June can deny ever taking the car. There is no real proof. It could easily have been stolen by a random person, it happens all the time. So what if she ran away from home? She has been of legal age for over a year.

But now it's much more likely that no one will call the police. Randy won't let Gail do it, considering what he has in the trunk. Nobody at home wants June talking to the authorities—not now, not ever. It occurs to her to call the cops about the body, but they would want to know how she ended up in Sacramento with this car, and turning herself in for grand theft auto sounds like a spectacularly bad idea.

She's seen enough cop shows to know that they'd get the truth out of her eventually, and even if she stayed out of jail, that road would end with her being sent back home to face Randy's wrath. No, there's only one option left: she just needs to skip this town and never look back.

First order of business is to ditch the Deathmobile. But she has to be careful; she has to do this the right way. The smell is going to get worse, which means the local cops will be all over this car soon enough. She needs to make sure there's no evidence linking her to the crime scene. With any luck, she'll be long gone by then, with enough plausible deniability to convincingly say she never came to Sacramento in the first place.

She finds a self-service car wash a few blocks away, across from a Taco Bell. After taking a black T-shirt out of her bag, she reaches in and pulls out her special bracelet, her father's words engraved inside: *To June, you will always be my little girl. Love, Dad.*

She never wears it anymore; after her father died, she stopped eating and lost so much weight that none of her jewelry fit. But today she needs her dad with her. He was the only one who ever made her feel safe, and it will take a special strength to get her through this day. Even though it's dangling loose from her right wrist, she tells herself she won't lose it. There must be at least one thing in this world that won't let her down.

She gets out of the car, thankful she has enough change for the power vacuum and hand washer.

Detailing the car doesn't take long. Randy has taken good care of it and kept it mostly clean; she just needs to make sure there aren't any stray hairs or fibers from her clothes on the upholstery or under the seats. Besides, it's nice to get outside and breathe some fresh air after driving all night.

An older red-headed woman in overalls and a long ponytail approaches and asks June if she needs anything. June bristles, but calms down when she realizes the woman is the attendant on duty and not some stranger accosting her for change.

"Hey, where's the nearest bus station?" June asks.

The woman scratches her head. "You know, I think it's down on L Street, that way." She points east across the intersection out front. "Near the mall."

"Thanks."

June finishes rinsing the soap off the car with a high-powered hose. Using the black T-shirt she took out earlier to avoid finger-prints, she opens the door and gets back in. She keeps the T-shirt wrapped around the steering wheel as she pulls out into traffic.

The red-headed lady was right; a Greyhound bus station is several miles down L Street. June passes it and continues east until she spots a shopping center with a giant sign announcing "Downtown Plaza." At the end of the street is a parking garage. June pulls in and parks on the third level.

Something has been scratching at the back of her mind: the duffel bag in the trunk. What's in it? It could be anything— maybe guns, drugs, or… Wouldn't it be crazy if it's full of money? It's possible; life is full of surprises.

If there's cash in that bag, well, that would make her next steps a whole lot easier. June closes her eyes, revulsion and desperation warring in her chest. Going into that trunk again is the last thing she wants, but she knows she doesn't have enough cash on hand to get very far. What if it's like in the movies? What if that bag is stuffed with bills? She has to make herself do this. The potential reward outweighs the disgusting smell and the risk.

She scans the parking lot, her eyes darting from corner to

corner. This level seems deserted, and the eerie silence suggests no cars are approaching. Stepping out, she paces back and forth along the length of the car, her footsteps echoing softly around her.

"Gotta do it, gotta do it," she repeats to herself, waving her arms around like she's psyching herself up for a high dive. "Don't look at the dead guy. He's already dead anyway, he won't mind. You can do this." She puts her backpack on the ground near the left wheel of the car.

She looks around again. Everything's still quiet. She takes a deep breath, lowers her head, and pops the trunk. Her eyes go wide as she realizes her big mistake—the duffel bag is *behind the body*. She will have to reach over the mangled corpse, maybe even touch him, to get to the bag. She reaches out for the trunk lid, about to give up, but the thought of a miraculous windfall makes her press on.

Her arm is almost too short. Stretching over the dead guy's curled, broken leg, she barely grabs the bag's drawstring and pulls as hard as she can. The bag lifts slightly, but falls back down.

"Shit."

She puts her hands on her knees and huffs for a moment. The futility of her situation crashes over her, quickly turning to anger. "Goddamnit." She is getting pissed off now. "I don't have time for this. I deserve that money."

She reaches in and yanks the drawstring back with all her strength. The bag scratches the dead guy's shoulder and comes bursting out of the trunk, showering the dank air with little flecks of dust and dead skin.

June is overcome with a bizarre feeling, a combination of the desire to celebrate and the need to throw up. On the verge of touching her face, she stops herself.

I just touched that bag, she thinks. It was in there with him.

The stench from the trunk makes her retch as she pulls the

bag open. It's filled with little plastic baggies, some with white powder and some with green stuff—must be weed. But this isn't like the skunk weed Bree had before. The stuff in these bags is thick and oily and bright green. June can already smell it through the plastic.

But no money. Fuck.

She doesn't want any drugs. Though she could try to sell these bags, she has no idea how to go about something like that, and she's in enough trouble already.

Tires squeak on the concrete. June glances back impulsively. Headlights are far off but coming this way. She reaches into the duffel bag and quickly rummages around to see if anything might be under all the drugs. You never know.

There, she can feel something. Shit yes. Piles of bills. She grabs a handful and tosses them into her backpack. Hurriedly, she makes three more grabs for cash before she thinks the approaching car is getting too close. She throws the duffel bag back into the trunk and barely slams the lid shut before an old orange Yugo drives by.

June holds her stomach for a few seconds, forcing herself to smile innocuously at the driver. When they are out of sight, she runs to the space in front of Randy's car and vomits; it's a lot, seemingly everything she's ever eaten in her life. After wiping her mouth with the cuff of her sleeve, she straightens up and tries to pull herself together.

"Got to get a move on," she whispers to herself.

She uses her trusty black T-shirt to wipe down the front seat one more time, then slams the car door shut with her hip. "*Hill Street Blues* got nothing on me."

She walks to the elevator at the far end of the building but stops herself before pressing the call button. That might leave a fingerprint. Better safe than sorry. She takes the stairs down and walks back along L Street.

Goodbye, Deathmobile.

. . .

The bus station isn't busy this early in the morning, which helps steady June's nerves. Even though she's making a clean getaway, she's still taking the biggest step of her life. She heads to the counter and asks for a Greyhound ticket to San Francisco. It seems as good a place as any. A big city with lots of people, where she can disappear into the crowd and buy some time to figure out how to survive. Besides, she's always wanted to see the ocean, and it's about as long a trip as she can handle right now. Though she won't count the newfound piles of cash until later when she's settled in, it must be enough to help her start a new life.

It has to be.

She's not kidding herself—she's scared shitless. With no one to help her, she's not sure how she'll make it in the long run. For the first time in her life, she is truly on her own, but her deep conviction is unwavering. She reminds herself of something she's heard before: nobody really has it all figured out anyway. Everyone's just making it up as they go along. So she gets on that bus and gives herself permission to start over, to make as many mistakes as it takes to get herself right.

Her only belongings are hastily packed clothes and a few essentials thrown into her backpack. She doesn't have a book or a magazine, not even a Walkman. Nothing to pass the time. But none of that matters to her now. There is enough to think about, and after the night she had (and the morning of horrors), she could use the sleep.

The bus pulls out and rumbles onto the freeway. June rolls up her jacket, tucks it behind her head, and closes her eyes. She doesn't need to look out the window; she's already seen enough of Northern California to last a lifetime.

She doesn't realize her special bracelet is missing until much later.

ABOUT THE AUTHOR

Jeff Silvey lives in Austin, Texas, with his wife and daughter. The city's blazing summers remind him that some kinds of heat you can't escape, no matter how far you drive. His fascination with stories of survival and the choices people make under pressure led him to create the Hear Me Baby series. This is his first novel.

Connect with him at jeffsilvey.com.

IF YOU LEAVE (A REVIEW)

If you connected with this story in any way, your support can make a big difference.

Reviews are the lifeblood of independent publishing—and even a short, honest review helps other readers discover the book. Whether you leave a few words or a full reflection, it truly means the world. So, please , please, please, let me get what I want… and leave a review on Amazon, Kobo, Goodreads, or wherever you purchased this book.

And if you're looking forward to what happens next… stay tuned. The story continues in *When the Lights*.

Thank you for reading—and for being part of this journey. This is only the beginning.

RESOURCES & SUPPORT

This book explores themes of trauma, abuse, and emotional struggle. If any part of June's story resonates with your own experience—or if you're facing anxiety, depression, or simply having a hard time—please know you are not alone. Help is available. Below are trusted, confidential resources that offer support, information, and a safe place to start.

United States:
RAINN (Rape, Abuse & Incest National Network)
24/7 Hotline: 1-800-656-HOPE (4673)
www.rainn.org

The National Domestic Violence Hotline
24/7 Hotline: 1-800-799-SAFE (7233)
Text "START" to 88788
www.thehotline.org

National Alliance on Mental Illness (NAMI)
HelpLine: 1-800-950-NAMI (6264)
www.nami.org
Free, confidential support and education for those affected by mental illness.

SAMHSA National Helpline
Substance Abuse and Mental Health Services Administration
1-800-662-HELP (4357) | 24/7, free, confidential
www.samhsa.gov
Offers treatment referral and information for mental health and substance use.

Mental Health America (MHA)
www.mhanational.org
Provides mental health screening tools, education, and community resources.

Crisis Text Line
Text HOME to 741741
www.crisistextline.org

Global:
• **International Directory of Domestic Violence Agencies**
www.hotpeachpages.net
• **UN Women Resources for Survivors of Violence**
www.unwomen.org

Befrienders Worldwide / Samaritans
www.befrienders.org
International network offering emotional support to prevent suicide. Includes links to Samaritans branches in the UK, Ireland, and other countries.

Open Counseling: Global Suicide & Mental Health Hotlines
www.opencounseling.com
A searchable directory of mental health crisis lines by country.

WHO Mental Health Resources
www.who.int / teams / mental-health-and-substance-use
Resources and links from the World Health Organization on mental health care access worldwide.

June's journey is only beginning. Read on for an exclusive preview of Book Two in the Hear Me Baby series.

1
INJECT THE VENOM

S UNRISE IGNITES the foothills of the Sangre de Cristo Mountains east of Santa Fe, bathing the Bellhaven Chambers Institute as it hums with early morning activity. Inside, those who work here are already sweating, not from the summer heat that will soon follow, but from the anxiety that begins each day.

No rest for the wicked.

Three hapless representatives from the Animal Testing Division are sweating more than most. They sit in a special meeting room near the top floor of the tower—stripped bare except for a monolithic black table over black tiles and sterile white walls. This is management's minimalist design, a stage set for high-stakes corporate theater.

An expansive window lets in sunlight, spotlighting a middle-aged man at the head of the table. He's impeccably dressed in a tailored gray suit, with thin horn-rimmed glasses framing cold, calculating eyes. His patrician face is taut with barely controlled anger, fingers tapping the tabletop in a steady rhythm of impatience.

The three technicians in white lab coats fidget in their chairs under his withering stare. The middle one twists his wedding ring around his finger, desperate for any distraction. He glances nervously at his colleagues flanking him—Carter, a younger man with darker skin, and Novak, an older woman with her blonde hair pulled back tightly—but finds no comfort in their equally worried faces.

Carter remains statuesque, his eyes averted, as if willing himself to disappear into the austere walls.

Novak, usually buried in her work, finds herself trapped in an unfamiliar pressure cooker. The situation feels surreal, like honor students called to the principal's office for something they didn't mean to do. She stares straight ahead, forcing a tight smile while yearning to escape back to the comfort of her lab.

The silence is suffocating. The man at the head of the table lets it drag on a beat too long before finally speaking.

"Let's cut to the chase, people. We have a problem." His voice is soft yet pointed. "Would one of you care to explain exactly what went wrong yesterday?"

The three lab technicians look at each other, a silent exchange thick with unease. The tech sitting in the middle clears his throat. "Well, sir, it seems that one of the... test subjects managed to get loose somehow." His voice wavers slightly.

The man in the suit raises an eyebrow. "Somehow? That's rather vague, don't you think, Mr. Keller?"

Keller swallows hard. "Yes, of course. What I mean is, we're still trying to determine how it happened. It appears the containment protocols may not have been followed correctly."

"Not followed correctly?" The words drip with icy disdain. "Quite an oversight when handling experimental subjects."

"Absolutely, sir. It was our mistake, and I take full responsibility as chief technician." Keller's face beads with sweat.

The man at the head of the table leans forward, pressing his fingertips together to form a steeple. "And where is this *test subject* now, exactly?"

"We, um… we don't know, sir. Once it got out into the ventilation system, we lost track of it. I have all available personnel searching the building, but so far…" Keller's voice trails off helplessly.

The man at the head of the table continues glaring at Keller. For a moment, his composed veneer seems to fracture, his eyes flashing with barely suppressed fury. But just as quickly, the polite smile returns.

"I see. Well, we certainly find ourselves in quite the predicament." He pauses, regarding each lab technician coolly. "Needless to say, this is unacceptable. That experiment was highly classified for a reason."

The technicians stare at the table, ashamed and terrified.

For the first time, the man raises his voice—not shouting, but letting it carry a deep, threatening resonance. "Project Chrysalis needs to get off the ground as soon as possible. The plan must be followed. There's more at stake here than just your jobs, understand?"

Keller hunches forward and mutters, "It's almost as if our lives depend on it." He means it as a joke, but when he looks up momentarily, the man isn't smiling.

Carter and Novak sit rigidly, caught in the confrontation. Keller's stammering apologies clash jarringly with the older man's cold composure. They exchange uncomfortable looks behind Keller's back, cringing at his stupidity.

Inside the Bell, information is carefully compartmentalized, parceled out on a need-to-know basis. Each team works on their small piece of the puzzle, blind to the bigger picture. Until today, the trio had operated under the illusion that they were just another cog in a larger, but mostly benign, machine.

That naive comfort now lies in ruins.

The man before them radiates menace, his quiet fury unmistakable. His tapping fingers promise dire consequences.

'I trust the three of you know what's at stake here?' The threat in his tone raises the hair on the back of their necks. They all nod dutifully.

"Good. Then I suggest you locate the subject and contain the situation. We can't have classified assets roaming around freely now, can we? I trust you three will handle this discreetly." He folds his hands. "Immediately."

"Of course, sir," Keller stammers. "Right away."

The technicians avert their gaze, the weight of their failure hanging over them like a guillotine. Keller loosens his tie with a trembling hand.

The man dismisses them with a wave toward the door.

"Let's go," Keller whispers to his colleagues.

They push back from the table, chairs scraping against the floor. With slumped shoulders, they shuffle toward the exit, crushed by the weight of their impossible task. Novak leans close to Keller, whispering urgently. He nods grimly as their footsteps echo down the empty hallway. The door closes behind them with an ominous thud.

The man punches a button on the table before him. A dial tone sounds. He dials a number.

"Watkins," a thin male voice says over the speakerphone.

"You know why I'm calling."

"Waste disposal?"

"Yes. Is it done?"

"No," Watkins replies. "I can't reach our guy. He's not returning my calls. I had someone drive by the house, but his car's not there. What do you want me to do?"

"Give him until the afternoon. Otherwise, his contract will have to be terminated. Either way, set everything in motion."

"Outside contractor. He was good though. Such a shame."

The man gets up from the table and strides down the corridor to a nondescript alcove that serves as a security hub.

A guard sits watching a wall of video screens. He looks up as the man enters.

"Boardroom Ten-A. Rewind to five minutes ago."

The guard nods and rewinds a tape in the VCR connected to his main monitor. He flips a switch. Another screen flickers to life, showing an overhead view of Boardroom Ten-A, just as the three technicians awkwardly rose from their chairs and shuffled toward the exit.

The man leans in. "Turn it up."

Grainy footage captures the female technician turning to Keller, strands of hair escaping from her tight bun as she whispers. The man leans in closer to the screen, grimacing as he strains to hear over the static.

"... and why didn't you tell him? About the one that exploded?"

Keller's reply is barely audible. "You know why." His lips move again, but the words are lost as they exit through the door.

The man has heard enough. He straightens and places a heavy hand on the security guard's shoulder. "Appreciated." He pivots to leave, then adds, "No disruptions, unless it's from Clarke."

"Got it, boss."

The man walks back to his office, lost in thought. *He was good though. Such a shame.*

Not a shame, the man thinks, but a necessity. The inevitable culling of the herd—those who are useful to us and those who will soon feed the worms.

2

(I'M LOOKING FOR) CRACKS IN THE PAVEMENT

FOR ROBERT SAMPSON, Thursday morning is a blur. The minimum day means shorter classes, and being the last day of school, it also means rambunctious kids lost in their own little worlds. They're beyond yielding to authority at this point, but it doesn't matter. They checked out months ago.

It's not long before he's standing before his fourth-period U.S. History class. Although better than third period, this class still leaves something to be desired. He's already resigned himself to letting the kids have a free period, no point in bothering today. The hangover from his late-night grading fiasco is gone, but his mind is still preoccupied—he can't stop thinking about June. This makes it the second day in a row she has missed school.

Between classes, Sampson decides to stretch his legs and get some fresh air. He tells himself that he's not just going out to look for June, though maybe she's here and just ditched his class. It happens. He knows he's not her favorite person. In the end, he doesn't care if she cut class; he just wants to talk to her.

He strolls along the open-air grounds on the east end of the campus. Green grass between the walkways provides some color in the washed-out atmosphere of the California heat. Groups of kids huddle together, chatting and laughing as they clean out their lockers along the outside of the building. Shouts and mindless chatter assault his ears from every direction; with teenagers everywhere, it's his own personal hell. Most of them look pale and worn out, but each one radiates pure joy. After all, freedom is only a few hours away.

In the crowd, his gaze rests on a striking blonde who looks like she's in her twenties, wearing a tight t-shirt and acid-washed jeans. Student teacher? No, he thinks, there was only one this year, and that was last semester. Wait, it's that girl—what's her name? Bree. Isn't she June's friend? He waves to get her attention. She looks away, then looks back sheepishly, apparently hoping he was waving to someone else. Nobody wants to talk to an unpopular teacher between classes on the last day of school.

Sampson waves again and walks over to her. The girl looks as if she would rather be anywhere else. If Sampson weren't so worried about June, he would find it amusing.

She is standing next to some guy with a Duran Duran haircut, his blond hair parted on the side, with long bangs hanging over his face. His "Choose Life" t-shirt is too big for him, making him look flat-chested and awkward. He looks down and mumbles something to her as Sampson approaches.

She turns to Duran Duran and sighs. "No, dude, it doesn't work that way. They came like this."

He glances down at her jeans, with bleached swirls and faded streaks creating a marbled effect across the fabric, then he looks up, his expression turning worried as he spots the teacher among them. Bree pivots to follow his gaze, feigning surprise, as if she hadn't just seen the teacher approaching. As if he wasn't just waving at her.

"Oh, hi!" Bree says excitedly, like the three of them have always been in a shining circle of friendship.

Sampson pauses; he doesn't know how to begin. For a split second, he's taken aback by the big-breasted blonde with her toothy smile and bag of tricks, but he's too focused on June to be swayed by that today. Lost in his thoughts, he stares at her silently.

Bree says, "Uh, can we help you?"

Sampson scratches his eyebrow. "Yeah, sorry. Hey, you're friends with June Addison, right?"

"Totally," Bree brightens, glad this isn't about her. "What's up? She in trouble again?"

"No, she's fine… I mean, I hope she's all right. Maybe you can tell me. She hasn't been in class lately. Is she sick?"

Duran Duran chimes in, sounding like an extra from *Fast Times At Ridgemont High*. "Dude, nobody's seen her for days." He glances down at the bright blue Swatch on his wrist. With a sudden lift of his chin, he flips his hair out of his eyes and turns to go, saying over his shoulder, "Gotta bail, later days."

"And better lays," Bree says under her breath. She looks sideways at Sampson and quickly adds, "You didn't hear that." She looks like she's about to leave as well.

Sampson has to stop himself from putting his hand on her shoulder. He raises his voice slightly to keep her attention but tries to sound casual. "So, you haven't seen her, then? You wouldn't happen to know where she is?"

Bree shrugs. "You know, I haven't talked to her since Monday. I called her house last night, and her mom said she wasn't home. Funny…" Her voice trails off as she looks down at her shoes.

Sampson raises his eyebrows for a moment, and when she doesn't continue, he asks, "What do you mean, funny?"

"Well, her mom sounded really weird."

"Weird how?"

"It was her voice. All low and scratchy and… strange. You know that Bruce Springsteen song on the radio? The 'Yeah America' one?"

Sampson knows the song she's talking about, and it's not a

pro-America song. Everybody always gets that wrong. "Born In The U.S.A." is about veterans having a hard time coming home from the Vietnam War and their struggles to cope with it all. But this is not the time to correct her. He doesn't want to rush Bree, but he knows that time is running out; they both need to get moving. So he says, "Yeah, I've heard it."

"There's a line in it somewhere: *Acting like a dog that's been kicked too much.* That's how she sounded. Distant, hollow, like she wasn't really there, you know? That's the only way I can describe it."

Sampson doesn't know what to think. What is she talking about? He doesn't have time to get into this now, so he glosses over it. "Huh? That does sound strange. Look, if you hear from June, let her know I need to speak with her, okay?"

"Will do."

"It's nothing bad."

"Yeah, sure. Whatever."

And with that, the girl in the tight t-shirt and acid-washed jeans saunters off down the hallway. Several boys turn their heads to watch her go.

The bell rings, drowning out the clamor of student voices. As the halls empty, Sampson stands alone, unable to shake the feeling that June's absence is much more complicated than he imagined.

3
RAT TRAP

THREE SHADOWS MOVE through the stairwell on the south side of the Bellhaven Chambers Institute, their footsteps muffled in the enclosed space. Ethan Keller pushes his glasses up—a habit that worsens with every passing hour. Novak matches his stride, her movements careful and efficient. Behind them, Carter glances over his shoulder every few seconds, checking for anyone following.

Reaching the third floor, Keller veers left.

"This way," he whispers, gesturing toward a maintenance corridor.

Novak frowns. "Ethan, where are you—"

"Cameras," Keller taps his temple. "Need somewhere off-grid."

Understanding passes between them without another word.

Keller tries three doors before finding one unlocked. The utility closet reeks of industrial cleaner and neglect. They squeeze inside, surrounded by towers of cleaning supplies and maintenance equipment. A single bare bulb casts their faces in harsh relief.

"We're completely fucked," Carter says, breaking the silence.

"Lower your voice," Novak says. "And that's not helping."

Keller paces the cramped space, taking three steps before turning back. "We need to think systematically. The subject couldn't have traveled far within the ventilation network. There are barriers, dampers."

"Unless it chewed through them," Novak says. "We've documented their capabilities."

Carter rubs his temples. "Why didn't you report the explosion, Keller? This is ten times worse now."

"Because we'd be dead already," Keller says, eyes sharp behind his lenses. "If management knew we lost two subjects, they'd have security escorting us to the basement right now." The implication hangs in the air, no need to elaborate on what happens in the basement.

Novak begins sorting through shelves, pulling down bottles, rags, and a length of PVC pipe. "We need to improvise. A trap, a net, something."

Keller nods, mind already calculating materials and designs. "Carter, grab that bucket and those cleaning gloves."

They work with desperate efficiency, assembling an improvised trap. Keller fashions a crude snare from electrical wire while Novak prepares a sedative solution from chemicals she had hid in her lab coat.

"This won't restrain it long," Keller says, testing his wire contraption. "But it might give us enough time to grab it."

Carter's face goes pale. "And what about the other one? The... remains?"

Keller adjusts his glasses again. "One disaster at a time."

Twenty minutes later, they emerge with their cobbled-together equipment. The hallway stands empty, but Keller feels unseen attention pressing against his skin. Somewhere, in some darkened room, security watches their every move.

The lab seems different upon their return—sterile in a way that feels threatening, as if the room itself knows their careers and lives balance on a knife's edge. Keller clears the central table and spreads building ventilation blueprints with unsteady hands.

"Here," he says, uncapping a red marker. "Junction points where the system branches." He circles several intersections, the marker squeaking against paper. "If it followed the air current, it would have moved upward through these shafts."

Novak leans over the blueprint, studying the layout. "No, that doesn't track. These subjects seek darkness and warmth. It would have descended toward the utility areas."

"You're both wrong," Carter interjects, tapping a different section. "Look at food sources. The cafeteria ventilation connects here. That's where I'd go if I were a hungry lab rat with enhanced cognitive function."

Keller's stomach tightens. "If it reaches the cafeteria during lunch hour…"

The thought remains unfinished. Public exposure would end everything.

"Junction C," Keller decides, circling it with three aggressive strokes. "It's a bottleneck. We start there."

An hour later, they position their first trap. It's crude, but it's all they have. At its center, Keller places a small dish of nutrient mix designed to be irresistible to their genetically modified creation.

They set up a closed-circuit camera connected to a bulky monitor in an adjacent maintenance room, threading the cable through a narrow gap in the wall. The grainy black-and-white image flickers occasionally. Carter can't stop checking his watch. Novak keeps unwavering focus on the fuzzy monitor, tapping the side of the unit when interference fills the screen with white noise.

Two hours pass like a slow-motion suffocation. The bait remains untouched. The trap sits empty.

"This isn't working," Novak says.

Keller stares at the untouched trap, a monument to their failure. On the monitor, snow flickers across the screen, mocking their efforts. His mind races, recalculating probabilities and searching for logical paths their creation might take.

"We need to think like it thinks," he murmurs. "Not where we would go, but where *it* would go."

Carter looks up, face ashen in the dim light. "We just tried that! Look, what if we can't find it in time? What happens then?"

Keller meets his gaze, the answer hanging unspoken between them. They all know what happens then. Reassignment to the basement, perhaps permanently.

4

THIS IS GOODBYE

THE SUN BEATS DOWN RELENTLESSLY on Vacaville High School's graduation ceremony as trumpets herald the occasion. Tugging at his collar, Sampson feels like he's being slowly roasted alive beneath his dark suit. He watches the symphonic band play, noting how the boys look visibly uncomfortable, their collars straining as they blow into French horns and trombones, punctuating the stately march with the occasional off-key note.

Row upon row of cap-and-gown-clad graduates sit before him, their faces beaming with pride and anticipation. A wry smile crosses Sampson's face as he contemplates the strange reality awaiting them. The intensity of teenage life, with all its drama, often seems more authentic than the mundane responsibilities of adulthood. These naive kids have no idea what lies ahead.

His gaze drifts over the assembled parents. Mothers fan themselves with commencement booklets, while nearby, a father wears a pained smile, likely pondering the looming specter of college tuition. Sampson wonders if the man's child will end up at Solano Community College. He considers how this transition might strain marriages that have focused solely on child-rearing. These parents, too, are unprepared for what lies ahead.

The commencement speaker, young and charismatic California State Senator Rachel Conrath, takes the stage. Her voice echoes across the football field, brimming with idealism. "Your parents have worked tirelessly to create a better world for you," she proclaims. "One day, the torch will pass to you. It will be your mission to improve the world for the next generation. And so the cycle continues, as it should."

Inwardly, Sampson scoffs. That's bullshit. These kids didn't choose this world, and neither did their parents. They found themselves here, just like everyone else, left to make the best of it and survive.

Senator Conrath introduces an acronym for her new foundation, HARMONY: Harmonization and Reformation for a Model New World Order. Sampson's pulse quickens. Did I hear that correctly? He glances around, but the other adults continue nodding, seemingly oblivious. Alarm bells ring in his mind: What kind of dystopian nightmare is this group proposing? And how is everyone falling for it? That acronym doesn't even work.

Meanwhile, many graduates chatter among themselves, some even high-fiving, paying little attention to the speaker. Sampson isn't surprised. They haven't paid attention to anything all year. He knows the only "better world" they're thinking about is how much weed they can score for this weekend's parties.

After the ceremony, Sampson navigates the bustling crowd, offering congratulations to the fresh-faced graduates. They beam with elation, reveling in their achievement. He maintains his distance, adhering to his no-hugging policy. As he watches them celebrate, a familiar melancholy creeps in. Are they as eager to forget me as I am to see them leave? Perhaps. Sampson isn't sure he even registers with them anymore. To them, he is already fading into a forgotten age.

His attention is drawn to a cluster of students gathered

around a tall blonde, her golden hair shimmering in the sunlight. Her radiant smile captivates everyone around her. She laughs, and they all join in. It's a rare moment of shared joy among these kids, who seldom laugh together in his class unless it's at someone else's expense.

With a jolt, Sampson recognizes the blonde as Bree, June's sole close friend. As the group disperses, Bree remains, clutching her diploma and turning in slow circles, her eyes darting between gaps in the sea of faces. Is she looking for June? No, he thinks, June is with her sick aunt. Surely Bree would know where June is.

Hesitating briefly, torn between avoiding Bree and maintaining his supportive teacher facade, Sampson approaches. Bree's face lights up, flushed with excitement. She moves to embrace him, but Sampson steps back, acutely aware of onlookers. He can't allow such familiarity in public.

Forcing a smile, he pats Bree's shoulder. "It's been quite a year," he says. "This was a good group. You're all going to do great things." The words feel hollow. Bree might succeed, but for the others? He has his doubts.

An older couple approaches, her silk Hermès scarf catching the light, his polished oxfords somehow immaculate even on the trampled grass. They move through the crowd like royalty at court, dispensing slight nods to the commoners in their path. Sampson surmises they must be Bree's parents. Wealth has a way of polishing people, he muses. At least on the surface.

Bree turns to Sampson, genuine appreciation in her eyes. "Thank you," she says warmly before turning to her parents.

Sampson starts to walk away, then hesitates. Before he can stop himself, he calls out, "Sorry about June."

Bree pivots, her brow furrowing. "What about June?"

Sampson clears his throat. "I know she's not graduating, but I'm sure she would have wanted to be here for you today. That's tough about her aunt. Must be hard for her."

"Her aunt? Which aunt?"

"I didn't catch her name." He recounts his visit to June's house, the conversation with her mother, the story of the sick aunt. He watches as Bree's expression morphs from puzzlement to worry.

"June's only aunt is Aunt Sylvia, on her dad's side," Bree says slowly, uncertainty coloring her voice. "But she passed away about five years ago. They said it was cancer."

Sampson wants to probe further, but Bree's father interjects, mentioning their lunch reservation. Bree nods, duty-bound, her attention drawn back to her family. The man extends his hand to Sampson with a polite nod. "Nice meeting you," he says, though no introductions were made.

As her family walks toward the parking lot, Bree glances over her shoulder one last time, a flicker of concern in her eyes before she composes herself, her smile returning.

Sampson stands amid the celebratory crowd, his mind reeling. This situation grows increasingly bizarre, a sense of helplessness gnawing at him. If even Bree doesn't know where June is…

He feels compelled to act, yet uncertainty paralyzes him. What can he do? What's even appropriate in a situation like this? He initially resented June for being in his class, but he never wished her harm. The thought of her disappearance, her face on missing person posters, sends a chill through him.

And why is her mother being so evasive? Why would she lie? Shouldn't she be more concerned about her missing daughter?

He realizes this is beyond his pay grade. Yet, he can't shake the urge to intervene. Perhaps it's time to involve the authorities.

As Sampson contemplates his next move, Cassandra Stevens approaches, arms outstretched. He sidesteps the embrace, forcing a pleasant expression.

"Congratulations, Cassandra. Enjoy your summer." His words sound empty; he can't help it.

Cassandra's eyes narrow, detecting his distraction. "Thanks, Mr. Sampson. Is something wrong?"

"I'm fine. Just have a lot on my mind." He dismisses her concern. "Take care of yourself out there."

With a nod, Cassandra rejoins her friends, their laughter fading as Sampson walks away.

He weaves through the mass of graduates and their families, his thoughts fixated on June. What happened to her? Is she in danger? The questions multiply, each more unsettling than the last.

After everything, he just hopes she's all right. Where could she be?

Don't miss what happens next.

Book 2 in the Hear Me Baby series, *When the Lights*, picks up right where Book 1 leaves off.

Coming soon.

Sign up at jeffsilvey.com to be the first to know when it's released.

www.ingramcontent.com/pod-product-compliance
Lightning Source LLC
Chambersburg PA
CBHW020409150626
46554CB00012B/505